Quinn's lean, muscled body quivered with tightly reined emotion

It took all Hope's willpower to hold back the urge to touch him. It was her last remaining defense to his unexpected invasion. Somehow she felt if she didn't cross that line, she could survive this encounter with her heart still intact.

Her gaze flew instinctively to Quinn's little niece and nephew. A drop of moisture dripped off her chin and she realized she was crying at the senseless injustice of a family being destroyed...and Quinn walking around with a price on his head and the guilt of his brother and sister-in-law's deaths on his soul.

Quinn.

A hundred questions formed in her mind. But only one seemed important. "What can I do to help?"

"Marry me."

Dear Harlequin Intrigue Reader,

Your summer reading list just wouldn't be complete without the special brand of romantic suspense you can only get from Harlequin Intrigue.

This month, Joanna Wayne launches her first-ever miniseries! You loved the Randolph family when you met them in her book *Family Ties* (#444). So now they're back in RANDOLPH FAMILY TIES, beginning with Branson's story in *The Second Son* (#569). Flesh and blood bind these brothers to each other—and to a mystery baby girl. All are her protectors...one is her father.

Familiar, the crime-solving black cat, is back in his *thirteenth* FEAR FAMILIAR title by Caroline Burnes. This time he explores New Orleans in *Familiar Obsession* (#570).

It had been Hope Fancy's dream to marry Quinn McClure, but not under a blaze of bullets! Are *Urgent Vows* (#571) enough to save two small children...and a lifelong love? Find out with Harlequin Intrigue author Joyce Sullivan.

With her signature style and Native American characters and culture, Aimée Thurlo revisits the Black Raven brothers from *Christmas Witness* (#544). In *Black Raven's Pride* (#572), Nick Black Raven would die to protect Eden Maes, the one-time and always love of his life. And he'd be damned before anyone would touch a hair on the head of *their* child.

So if you can handle the heat, pull the trigger on all four Harlequin Intrigue titles!

Sincerely,

Denise O'Sullivan
Associate Senior Editor
Harlequin Intrigue

Urgent Vows
Joyce Sullivan

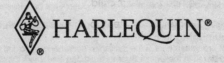

HARLEQUIN®

TORONTO • NEW YORK • LONDON
AMSTERDAM • PARIS • SYDNEY • HAMBURG
STOCKHOLM • ATHENS • TOKYO • MILAN • MADRID
PRAGUE • WARSAW • BUDAPEST • AUCKLAND

ISBN 0-373-22571-7

URGENT VOWS

Copyright © 2000 by Joyce David

Printed in U.S.A.

ABOUT THE AUTHOR

Joyce credits her lawyer mother with instilling in her a love of reading and writing—and a fascination for solving mysteries. She has a bachelor's degree in criminal justice and worked several years as a private investigator before turning her hand to writing romantic suspense. A transplanted American, Joyce makes her home in Aylmer, Quebec, with her handsome French-Canadian husband and two casebook-toting kid detectives.

Books by Joyce Sullivan

HARLEQUIN INTRIGUE
352—THE NIGHT BEFORE CHRISTMAS
436—THIS LITTLE BABY
516—TO LANEY, WITH LOVE
546—THE BABY SECRET
571—URGENT VOWS

Don't miss any of our special offers. Write to us at the following address for information on our newest releases.

Harlequin Reader Service
U.S.: 3010 Walden Ave., P.O. Box 1325, Buffalo, NY 14269
Canadian: P.O. Box 609, Fort Erie, Ont. L2A 5X3

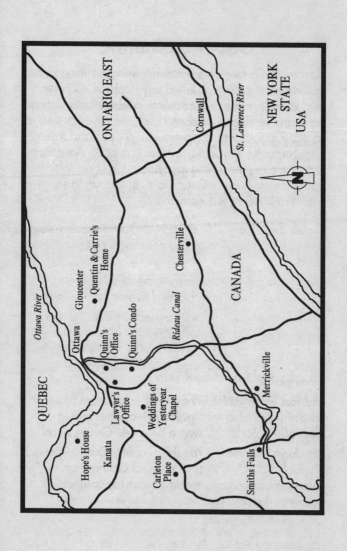

CAST OF CHARACTERS

Quinn McClure — This counterfeit expert is certain his identical twin was killed in his place. Can he find a mother for his brother's children before the hit man rectifies his error?

Hope Fancy — Always a fiancée and never a bride. Would a jinx and a hit man prevent her from marrying her first love?

Mercy and Bernardo — Who had hired this hit man and his sidekick?

Asian Syndicate — They feared Quinn was coming too close to identifying the principals of their credit card ring.

Hugh Simons — The mastermind of this payday counterfeit check ring blamed Quinn for his arrest.

Ross Linville — Quinn's investigation into the stock certificates he'd counterfeited to use as collateral for a bank loan had tarnished his family's sterling name. Now he'd skipped bail. Was he plotting revenge?

Adrian Burkhold — When Quinn exposed him as the head of a rare gold coin counterfeiting operation, Burkhold swore he'd see Quinn dead.

Dr. Juan Chavez — Was this wealthy Dominican Republic doctor trying to prevent Quinn from telling a packed courtroom about his counterfeit medical diplomas?

For Jeannie, who found her Sha'ul.
May you live happily ever after.
Mazel tov.

ACKNOWLEDGMENTS

A serendipitous meeting with two charming
and debonair gentlemen was the inspiration for this
book. I would like to extend my gratitude to
Jean-Claude Doré, Forensic Counterfeit Examiner
and Robert Fawcett, Forensic Document Examiner,
of Counterfeit & Forgery Prevention Inc. for sharing
the details of their fascinating work.

Thanks also to Inspector Al Misner, RCMP Forensic
Ident Services Ottawa; T. Lorraine Vassalo,
Criminologist; Detective-Sergeant Bill Bowles, Ontario
Ministry of the Solicitor General and Correctional
Services; Detective-Sergeant Clyde Dyck,
Chief Firearms Officer, Ontario Ministry of the
Solicitor General and Correctional Services;
Dee Barlow, ADT Security Systems Canada;
Lawyers Robert Lewis and Glen Kealy; Jackie Oakley,
Ottawa-Carleton Regional Police;
Dr. Stephen W. Maclean; Karen Robertson;
Kathryn Young-Davies; Pat and Linda Poitevin;
and Judy McAnerin

Any mistakes are my own.

Prologue

The electronic beeper on his wristwatch sounding noon roused Mercy from sleep, his heart pounding, the blood pumping through him and rushing to his head.

Had the bodies been discovered yet? Mercy scratched his private parts, then rolled over and grappled for the TV remote on the bedside table. The hand that had been so steady last night, so deadly, now trembled with anticipation.

The morning news had been ungratifying—not one mention of the killings. But surely, now there'd been time.... The set came on with a burst of color and sound in the darkened motel room.

A satisfied smile twisted his mouth as the thin-lipped, tight-assed, primly suited anchorwoman gazed solemnly into the camera, her expression conveying both sympathy and outrage as she segued into the lead story.

"Residents in Gloucester are in shock today over the gruesome discovery of the bodies of a man and a woman shot to death in their home. A neighbor spotted the couple's three-year-old daughter through a kitchen window and became suspicious when it appeared the girl was unsupervised. Police are not commenting on whether it was a botched burglary or a murder/suicide. A toddler was also found in the home. He was unharmed. Names will not be released until the next-of-kin have been notified.''

Mercy flipped her the bird and switched to another Ottawa station, just catching the tail end of the story. He got some satisfaction from seeing footage of the neighbors huddled outside the house. The fear stamped on their faces made his chest swell. Damn straight they should be afraid. Mercy was no one anyone wanted to mess with—not if they didn't want to find themselves six feet under or reduced to dust in a fancy bottle.

This station reported no names were being released, too. Mercy threw the remote against the wall. If he was lucky he'd get positive confirmation on the evening news, then he could blow off this town filled with politicians and civil servants squabbling over pay increases and tax cuts to medical and social programs. He took a deep breath and forced himself to relax. He'd followed the bastard home from the office, and the mail piled in a basket on a table in the living room had been addressed to Q. D. McClure. The confirmation was just a technicality. Necessary paperwork.

He was on his way into the bathroom when his digital cellular phone rang. "Yeah?"

He recognized the dry, raspy voice. "Has the job been completed?"

"Last night. Just waiting for positive ID. His old lady woke up so I ended up poppin' her, too."

"Don't expect extra. Just fax me a copy of the newspaper report and I'll have the money wired directly to your account. It's been a pleasure doing business with you." The line went dead.

Mercy grunted and shook his head, remembering how the woman had stirred, her blond head lifting from the pillow…and how he'd popped her before the scream could rise from her throat.

His body tightened. Yeah, the pleasure was all his.

Chapter One

"It should have been me. Not them," Quinn Mc-
Clure told the solemn-faced lawyer who'd agreed to
this cloak-and-dagger meeting in a fast-food restaurant. But then, never in a million years could Quinn
have imagined himself, with two young children in
tow, on the run from a hit man.

Of medium height and average build, wearing a
conservative gray suit topped with a black overcoat,
Tom Parrish glanced up from the pages of the last
will and testament of Quinn's brother, Quentin Mc-
Clure. Parrish was sharp, with a glint of ingrained
caution evident in his hazel eyes. "I'm sorry for your
loss. I'll do whatever I can to help."

Quinn nodded. He'd never felt so numb. His
thoughts seemed disconnected from his body, neither
fully registering the actions of the other. Or maybe it
was that the part of him which had always been
linked to his identical twin brother, Quentin, was irretrievably severed. And yet, Quinn had to think. Had
to resist sinking into the black whirlpool of grief that

had opened in the pit of his stomach. He had to do what was best for the children before he hunted down the bastard who'd gunned down Quentin and Carrie in their sleep.

A Mountie always gets his man. Even ex-Mounties.

Parrish set Quentin's will aside on the table and picked up Carrie's. Quinn's fingers trembled as he tried unsuccessfully to blot the horror of identifying his brother and sister-in-law's bodies from his mind. Tried not to remember the last joking conversation he'd had with Quentin when his brother had dropped by Quinn's office Wednesday evening to pick up the ticket Quinn had bought him for a Senators' hockey game.

Parrish's narrow brow furrowed. "Both wills appoint a Charles Duncan as the children's alternative guardian."

"That's Carrie's dad," Quinn explained, struggling to keep his teeming emotions from his tone. "He had a debilitating stroke just after Christmas. He's in a nursing home in Nova Scotia. I guess Quentin and Carrie never got around to selecting someone else—"

Quinn swallowed hard, unable to continue. Heat seared the backs of his eyelids. He hadn't called the nursing home yet. He couldn't bear to think of Charlie being told such news by a stranger. Couldn't bear to think of Charlie's grief at learning his only child and her husband were dead. That his grandchildren were orphaned.

Twenty-six hours had passed since Quinn had received the horrible call early yesterday afternoon informing him that Quentin's and Carrie's bodies had been found in their home. He told himself that he'd made it through the first horrific day and could make it through another. He'd been an RCMP officer too long not to immediately suspect the grisly truth when he'd arrived on the scene. It looked like a professional hit. Forced entry in a neighborhood that hadn't seen a break-and-enter in over three years. Victims shot at close range with a .22 semiautomatic. None of the neighbors had heard a sound, and there was no sign of the spent casings, which indicated the hit man had used a silencer. Not a damn thing was taken. A quick in-and-out job. Quentin's wallet and Carric's purse weren't even touched.

Damn. It was his fault.

Every day of his life he'd live with the torturous knowledge that the hit man had followed Quentin home by mistake. Quentin hadn't had an enemy in the world. But Quinn had a long list of enemies—all of them criminals, and not one of whom appreciated his efforts to toss their sorry asses in prisons all over the globe for counterfeiting anything from currency, credit cards, checks and travel documents to high-end designer clothes, salon products and stuffed toys.

A forensic examiner specializing in counterfeit detection and prevention, Quinn had left the RCMP at the invitation of Oliver Wells, a forgery specialist who was ready to retire from the RCMP and wanted to open up a private consulting firm. Their clients were many and varied: government agencies, financial institutions, insurance companies, law-enforcement agencies, private-investigation and security agencies, and private companies all over the world sought out their technological expertise to deter fraud and their investigative skills to combat it.

Once Quinn had realized his twin's death was a professional hit, it hadn't taken him long to provide the Ottawa-Carleton Regional Police with a short list of crime syndicates and individuals who possessed the motivation and the resources to order a hit on him. Not that he thought a list would do much good when the hit had likely been ordered by someone outside the country.

Quinn had a more straightforward means of finding out who'd hired the hit man. He planned to extract the information from the bastard when he came back to rectify his mistake. Oh yes, Quinn knew beyond a shadow of a doubt that the cold-blooded killer would return to finish the job he'd been hired to do. And when he did, Quinn planned to be ready and waiting. But first, he had to make sure that Quentin and Carrie's children would be well taken care of in the event something happened to him.

Quinn cast a watchful eye toward the play area of the restaurant where his friend, Gordon Swenson, who'd arranged this meeting with the lawyer, was supervising nineteen-month-old Kyle and three-year-old Melanie's antics in the ball room. Then he panned the room, checking for anyone or anything that seemed unusual or out of place. The police hadn't released the names of the victims to the press yet, but that didn't mean the hit man hadn't already been alerted to his error.

Tom Parrish carefully placed Carrie's will on top of Quentin's and aligned the corners. "Given what Gord has told me over the phone about your circumstances, Quinn,'' he ventured in a low tone, ''the best way to ensure that your niece and nephew don't end up wards of the Crown—in the unfortunate event of your death—would be for you to marry and appoint your wife as their guardian in your will. As their aunt, your wife would be considered a relative of the children and it's unlikely the court would choose not to uphold your request, particularly since there would be no opposing claim. Have you been seeing anyone lately you might consider marrying?''

Quinn shook his head. He'd only ever considered marriage once in his life—very briefly—and that was a decade ago. ''The ladies I occasionally date aren't the nurturing types. Besides, Kyle and Mel deserve a mother who'll love them as much as Carrie did and be willing to raise them on her own if she has to. From a security perspective, the children would be safer with a stranger. We don't know the resources behind whoever ordered the hit. Once they realize I've gone into hiding with the children, they'll start digging into my background looking for people who might be in a position to help me out. That's why I came to you instead of my own lawyer. It minimizes the risk of discovery because there are no links to trace.''

Quinn rubbed his jaw, feeling the rasping bite of the stubble on his chin. ''Gord told me you come from a big extended family. I don't suppose you know any single women willing to take on two kids?''

Parrish looked thoughtful for a moment. ''My wife will probably string me up for suggesting this, but one of her sisters runs a day care out in Kanata. She's a terrific person. Funny, caring. Loves kids. My daughters are five and two and they adore her. She's definitely the kind of person you think should have kids of her own, but she lost her fiancé a few years ago in a car accident and she's pretty much given up on the idea of having a family. You could talk to her, see if she's willing to help you. To my knowledge she's not seriously involved with anyone, but she likes to keep her personal life private. It drives my wife nuts.''

"I'd make it worth her while. Money won't be a problem."

Parrish didn't bat an eyelash. "Since I'm your lawyer and she's my sister-in-law, I'll make sure she's adequately provided for. But the only reason she'd do it is because she loves children. I just don't want her to get hurt."

"I'll take every precaution necessary to make sure that doesn't happen. You have my word. I only plan to stay long enough for the kids to bond with her." Quinn couldn't believe he was even talking about marrying a perfect stranger. "How soon could we be married if your sister-in-law accepts my proposal?"

"Monday at the earliest. The two of you would need to go down to city hall and apply for a marriage license in person. There's no waiting period or blood test required in the province of Ontario. Unfortunately, judges no longer perform civil ceremonies in this region, but I can make all the necessary arrangements with a nondenominational minister and draft your will once you talk to Hope."

Hope? Quinn's heart thumped queerly in the numb

cavern of his chest. "Your sister-in-law's name is Hope?"

"Yes, Hope Fancy, if you can believe it."

Quinn couldn't. He'd never thought he'd hear that quaint, old-fashioned name again.

Parrish removed a cell phone from the pocket of his overcoat. "Maybe I should call her and tell her I'm sending a visitor her way."

"I'd rather you didn't," Quinn said sharply. Too sharply. He softened the edge to his request, realizing Parrish didn't have a clue he'd known Hope long ago. "Cell phone calls can be picked up on scanners. I'd prefer a letter of introduction and directions to her place. I'll take care of the explanations myself."

Quinn just hoped she wouldn't hate him even more for what he was about to do.

So much for eloping with David and living happily ever after!

Hope dropped her suitcase containing the silky jewel-toned lingerie she'd bought for her honeymoon on the mat inside the darkened foyer and sagged against the firm panels of the front door as the humiliation she'd been holding back for the last hour and a half burst from her heart in a guttural moan.

Why on earth had she been jinxed with the uncanny ability to pick the wrong men to fall in love with? As if two broken engagements and the death of one fiancé in the last ten years weren't hard enough for a woman to endure, she could now add being jilted at the altar to her list of challenging life experiences.

Her chin jutted up stubbornly in her own defense.

Not that those two broken engagements were anything to be ashamed of. She had loved Quinn McClure with her whole heart and soul, and the week they'd been engaged had been tantamount to heaven on earth. If his father hadn't died, her life might have been so different.... She hadn't dated anyone else for over a year and a half, hoping that Quinn would somehow come to his senses.

But Quinn hadn't and she'd met Steven. Her engagement to the Realtor had been a mistake. He was everything Quinn wasn't, which was the problem. Though charming and successful, he simply wasn't Quinn. Telling Steven the truth had been the right, though painful, thing to do. Hope ran into him now and again in parks and at Ottawa's many museums and had met his wife and his growing family: two daughters and a third child on the way. No, that had worked out for the best because two years later she'd met Matthew, a veterinarian, whose quiet strength, Nordic good looks and infinite patience had helped her recover from the damage Quinn had done to her heart. They'd dated for over a year before Matthew had asked her to marry him. Hope's only regret was that she had insisted on a long engagement to give them time to truly get to know each other. He'd died in a car accident three weeks before their Valentine's Day wedding.

Four years had passed since Matthew's death and Hope had decided she'd had quite enough of love until David Randall had entered her life six months ago.

Thank God she hadn't told anyone she and David

were eloping tonight—not her family, not even Marie Elizabeth, her closest friend since grade school.

David's suggestion that they elope, which had seemed so sensitive and romantic at the time of its offering, had saved her from being subjected to yet more sympathetic looks and exclamations of "Not again!" Kanata was a small town and people had long memories.

Though, of course, David's secretiveness had garnered him precisely what he'd wanted...he would still be a groom, only the louse would be married to his old flame Susan, who'd driven up from Toronto to stop him from marrying her.

Hope had no idea how Susan had learned of their plans, but she'd made quite a dramatic scene, rushing into the quaint stone chapel wearing a sleeveless, silver-blue frothy confection and glittering silver sandals that put Hope's demure and practical blush-pink suit and white pumps to shame. Susan's Cinderella-gold mane had flowed gracefully onto her tanned shoulders, her bottle-green eyes liquid with tears as she'd professed her undying love for David and pleaded with him to marry her instead.

Hope had let them have each other and counted herself lucky she hadn't wasted another thousand dollars on a fancy wedding dress for a ceremony that would never be performed. At least, she'd been able to *wear* her wedding dress this time.

Figuring she'd indulged in enough self-pity, she wiped the tears from her cheeks and felt along the wall for the light switch. She blinked as the soft hazy pools cast by the table lamps brightened the redbrick Victorian farmhouse's cheery front parlor. The lace curtains, the wide varnished pine floorboards, the rose-patterned wool area rug, the plump cushions lining the blue chintz sofa and the photographs cluttering the walls, soothed the hollow ache in her heart with their homeyness. The truth was, she had everything she needed: her health, a home, a successful business and children in her life...even if they weren't *her* children.

Besides, she was beginning to think husbands were more trouble than they were worth.

Hope kicked off the white pumps, burrowed into a corner of the sofa and covered herself with a rainbow-hued afghan she'd made several frigid winters ago. It had the sweet nostalgic scent of the children who played with it day in and day out, used it for a blanket, a tent or a king's robe. Hope's jaw ached as she clamped back on a fresh crop of tears stinging her eyes.

Maybe somebody up there was trying to tell her something.... Her thirtieth birthday was a dim memory. Her younger sisters Grace, Faith, Charity and Patience were all married and had children—some of them teenagers. And her best friend Marie Elizabeth, who'd divorced her first husband, was happily ensconced in her second marriage and busy blending two families together.

The telling silence of the empty house she and Matthew had bought forced Hope to acknowledge painfully that she was a crummy judge of male character. She'd have been much better off if she'd turned down David's dinner invitation when they'd been introduced to each other by a mutual friend at a coffee shop, and hadn't let herself be swayed by the boxes of raspberry jelly donuts he'd leave on her porch. But he'd seemed so perfect—a stable and dependable accountant who shared her family values.

However, there was plenty of contentment to be found in the fact she was a wonderful aunt, sister, daughter and friend, and made a valuable contribution in the nurturing of all the children who passed through the doors of Home Away from Home, her day- and night-care center. She could buy her own jelly doughnuts.

An early spring wind sighed heavily in the eaves, the rafters cracking and groaning as if agreeing with her decision. The throaty purr of a motor turning in the drive and the pinging of gravel crunching beneath tires mingled with the sound of the wind. Hope saw a twin beacon of headlights swing across the front window for an instant.

Oh no!

Her pulse pounded through the veins in her wrist as she lifted the lace panel and peered out into the night, hoping David hadn't followed her. Another dramatic scene she did *not* need.

She briefly considered turning off the lights and refusing to answer the door, but that would make her a coward. David was an adult. He had the right to choose whom he wished to marry. She just didn't want to hear any explanations that were supposed to make her feel better—and ease his guilt!

The yard security lights flashed on as the car drew to a halt, illuminating the driveway and the rain-withered, misshapen snowmen rising like ghostly creatures from the snowdrifts still covering her front lawn. Winter hadn't completely released her grip on the land.

A figure emerged from the driver's side. A man. But he seemed taller and more imposing than David, his shoulders seeming to take on superhuman proportions. Or perhaps that was her imagination? No, it wasn't David. This man had a thick, full head of black hair that gleamed with a bluish sheen beneath the light. He wasn't one of the fathers or stepfathers of her routine charges either. But something about him seemed vaguely familiar.

His every footstep rattled the wet loose gravel until he hit the red-brick path that wound up to the house, then he moved soundlessly, almost stealthily, pausing with obvious uncertainty on the rim of the sagging porch as if he weren't sure he'd found the right address. But an enormous colorful placard in the shape of a house, with children playfully peeping out of windows, was impossible to miss at the end of the driveway. Was he just someone asking for directions?

She saw him look back over his shoulder toward the white sport utility vehicle. Unease slithered down the bones of her spine. Hope dropped the curtain and clambered off the sofa, not for the first time wishing she had a dog—something big with an intimidating growl. But a lot of toddlers were scared of dogs, and she didn't want any child under her roof to feel anything but happy and safe. Besides, she'd developed a mother's fine sense of hearing and wakened immediately at the slightest sound.

Telling herself she was being ridiculous, Hope quickly and silently moved to the kitchen and grabbed her cordless phone off the end of the counter as the man's knuckles thumped against the screen door. Whoever he was, at least he'd obeyed the instructions on the card posted over the doorbell requesting people not to ring the bell as children could be sleeping.

"Just a minute," she called softly. None too gently, she wrestled her suitcase into the crowded hall closet, then engaged the security latch at the top of the door which prevented her young charges from sneaking out to climb the old apple tree the moment her back was turned.

She flicked the porch light on. Phone clasped firmly in her damp hand and her finger poised to dial at the first sign of trouble, she eased open the door. The bolt slid along the latch and caught, granting her a six-inch crack through which she could speak without appearing rude.

She had an unfettered view of a chest that rose and expanded like a rough-hewn peak to the jagged thrust of a granite jaw and lean cheeks. Slate-gray eyes, glinting with uncertainty down the blade of a sharp, chiseled nose, impaled her. Disbelief slapped her in the face.

Hope dropped the phone, oblivious to the clattering it made as it hit the floor. She must be dreaming. The man in black jeans and the black anorak zipped up to his chin had to be a figment of her imagination. "Quinn?"

He dug his fingers into his hair, sweeping it back from his broad forehead. His words were low and strained. "I'm sorry to barge in on you like this unannounced. But I need you. It's an emergency."

He needed her? Surely this was a joke. No, a

nightmare. Any moment now she'd wake up with a start on her couch, but Hope didn't want to wake up. Quinn was gazing at her with the same hungry intensity he'd looked at her with ten years ago; as if he were devising a plan to sweep her off to a secluded spot where he would promptly persuade her that they both had on far too many clothes.

The thought of Quinn naked, making love to her, brought a sharp stab of pain to her abdomen. "I'm sorry, I can't," she murmured, resisting his intrusion into her heart. Not tonight. Not ever again.

He stuck the toe of his boot in the door, preventing her from closing it in his face. "Please, Hope. Your brother-in-law, Tom Parrish, sent me. He thought you could help me out of a jam."

Hope didn't even know that her brother-in-law knew Quinn. Tom and her sister Faith hadn't met until years after Quinn had gone back to the RCMP Fraud Squad in Toronto. "What does Tom have to do with this—?" She broke off as the piercing wail of a child's cry split the air—a wail of fear that pierced Hope's heart. A child. He had a child. After what he'd told her....

"Just a sec." He leapt off the porch in a bound, calling over his shoulder, "That's Kyle. Once he gets going, he's sure to wake up Melanie."

Kyle? Melanie?

Not one child. Two. The man who'd broken her heart when he told he'd never be a family man had children. And, obviously, a wife.

Damn him. It was too much. She supposed now he wanted her to baby-sit. It was almost laughable.

As Quinn swooped down on the car like a hawk

upon a mouse, Hope unlocked the front door and stepped onto the porch in her nylons, shivering as the cold from the planks bored into the soles of her feet.

Quinn's imposing back was hunched over the open car door. She opened her mouth to call out to him that despite what Tom had told him, she was closed until after Easter, when he straightened and Hope saw the squirming legs of a restless toddler in pastel-green pajamas, and the pale oval of a tiny face, shaking in protest at being held in his father's arms. Quinn's expression matched that of his son's: complete and total frustration, and Hope's protest died on her lips. There'd been a shower earlier in the day. She hoped Quinn still had enough presence of mind to put a blanket around his son. And what did it matter if she baby-sat Quinn McClure's children? He had said it was an emergency, and that Tom had sent him. She could at least hear him out.

"Ou-t!" A second cry from the car's interior drifted toward Hope on a fresh gust. Hope saw a windmill of churning legs as Quinn firmly tucked Kyle under one arm and rounded the car to the other side, where he opened the door and reached into the car with his free arm to assist the unseen Melanie. Hope decided he could use a second pair of hands.

Running into the parlor, she stepped into her pumps, then swept the afghan off the couch. The screen door slapped behind her as she hurried down the porch steps, the wind tugging her long hair in all directions.

She slowed at the gravel drive, picking her way carefully in her pumps. Judging by the sound of things, Quinn wasn't any closer to having his children under control.

"Where's Mommy? I want Mommy! *Now!* My hair's caught—and it hurts!" Hope heard the gasping windup of a sob in the making.

Quinn was patient, his voice strained, his body blocking Hope's view of his daughter. "Mommy's not here, Mel-Mel. But I am. Now hold still so I can get your hair untangled and get you out of this car seat. Who designs these things anyway— Kyle, ouch! Those are my ribs, pal. If you keep kicking like that, I'm going to drop you and you'll get hurt."

Melanie let loose a torrent of agonized howls as if to point out that she, unlike her brother, was in actual pain and must be dealt with immediately.

Afghan in hand, Hope offered to help.

Quinn backed out of the car and straightened, then sagged against the side of the vehicle, Kyle still trying to twist himself free from the restraint of his father's forearm. Quinn's relief was obvious. His expression held a tightly reined desperation that shook Hope to the core. "Maybe you could loosen Mel's hair for me and I'll take the kick-boxer inside. He sorely needs a diaper change. Then we can talk?"

"Mm-hmm." Hope grasped one of Kyle's sturdy little feet and dredged up her brightest smile, her nose wrinkling at the indelicate odor wafting from the toddler's clothing. "Hi! You must be Kyle. I've got a rainbow blanket to warm you up. Have you ever been hugged by a rainbow?"

Blue-gray eyes, ringed with black lashes, widened beneath finely drawn wisps of brows. Hope experienced a pang of envy. Kyle's hair was as dark as his father's. Tousled curls framed his rounded brow where a boo-boo was healing. The toddler stilled almost instantly as she tucked the blanket firmly around his warm, compact body and the iron-hard band of Quinn's arm. "There, nice and cozy now, aren't you?"

"Thanks," Quinn murmured. Hope felt her cheeks heat as his measuring gaze slid over her. It was not the sort of look she expected a father of two to brandish about—unless he was divorced?

Another howl from Melanie, this one, degrees more pitiful than the first, had Hope crawling into the toy-littered car, which smelled like new upholstery, male cologne, Kyle's soiled diaper, and spilt apple juice, toward a three-year-old with chocolate-brown eyes and silky amber hair that fell in angel curls past the shoulders of her heart-dotted purple sweat suit. "My goodness, Melanie," she intoned softly, giving the little girl a chance to get accustomed to her and her voice. "You poor lamb, looks like you've got your fleece all caught up in this funny-looking fence. My name's Hope. Would it be all right with you if I untangle you?"

Melanie sniffled, and after a moment's hesitation demanded, "What's feece?"

"It's a sheep's hair."

Melanie stretched a hand up to Hope's face and stroked the hair at her temple, her touch soft and tentative. "Are you a fairy? Mommy says fairies wear flowers in their hair."

Flowers? What was she talking about...? Oh, good heavens! Hope followed Melanie's fingers, her face reddening when she found a spray of baby's breath still lingering in her hair from the fiasco of her wedding. She pulled out the flowers and handed them to Melanie.

"No, I'm not a fairy," she said lightly. "Just always a fiancée. But my friend the robin told me I'd be having a little lamb come for a visit tonight so I was saving it for you."

Melanie beamed.

"We'll put it in your hair *after* we get you free." Hope expertly manipulated the straps and the release button of the car seat, then made short work of the snarl that had caused all the ruckus and tucked the delicate white flowers behind Melanie's left ear. "Lovely."

"I'm always a fiancée, too."

Hope rolled her eyes and lifted the little girl out of her car seat to help her on with the bubble-gum-pink jacket she found on the front passenger seat beside a smaller navy jacket with red and yellow stripes on the sleeves, and a diaper bag. A quick glance over her shoulder toward the house told her Quinn was letting himself in the front door.

Hope grabbed Kyle's jacket and slipped the diaper bag over her shoulder, then reached for Melanie's hand. "Come on. It's much too cold to let a little lamb like you frolic in the fields. How about you come in the house for a snack while I talk to your daddy?"

"Daddy's here?"

To Hope's surprise, Melanie's eyes filled with tears. She wondered if the preschooler was afraid Quinn had left without telling her so.

"Your daddy's in the house, lamb. With Kyle.

And we'd better hurry because any second he's going to figure out he forgot the diapers in the car.''

Melanie's face transformed into a wreath of smiles. She scampered up the front walk at full tilt, calling out, "Daddy! Daddy! I'm here! I knew you weren't dead!"

What on earth? Hope's blood ran cold. Had she heard correctly? She hurried after Melanie as fast as her high heels would allow her.

Melanie yanked on the screen door as Quinn opened the front door. Melanie latched on to his legs. "Oh, Daddy! You're not dead."

Quinn seemed to stagger under her assault. The flash of pain that whitened his features and turned his eyes into gray pits of agony halted Hope in her tracks on the porch steps. Even as Quinn was pulling Melanie up into his arms and cradling her tightly against his chest, she knew who these children were. Tears blurred her eyes as Quinn said raggedly, "Oh, baby. I'm Uncle Quinn. Not Daddy. Daddy's dead. I'm so sorry."

Melanie's face twisted, and a heart-wrenching sound echoed from her throat.

Hope's heart felt as if it were being punctured by her ribs. *The poor darling lamb!* Her hand fluttered to her mouth as Melanie turned brown eyes glaring with accusation at her.

"You lied. You said Daddy was here."

Hope's voice trembled. "Oh, sweetie. I didn't know. I thought he was your daddy. I'm so sorry I upset you. I hope you can forgive me."

Melanie's lower lip jutted out belligerently.

Quinn pressed a kiss on his niece's cheek. "It's

not her fault, Mel-Mel. Kyle woke up before I could tell Hope why we're here.''

Melanie fingered the baby's breath in her hair. ''Does this mean I'm not always a fancy eater?''

Quinn's brow crinkled. ''Huh?''

Hope leapt to his rescue. ''Never mind. It's a girl thing. Of course, lamb. You're a fairy fiancée. Now how about that snack I promised? Poor Kyle must really be feeling the need for a clean diaper about now.'' She handed Quinn the diaper bag.

''I don't wear diapers,'' Melanie announced in a superior tone. ''I'm not a baby.''

''Kyle?'' Quinn whirled around and strode into the house, Melanie still clutched in his arms, the diaper bag banging against his thighs. ''Oh God. I forgot about him.'' He turned toward the small downstairs bedroom Hope used for a change room and her kids' cubby holes.

''He's not there,'' Hope said, hearing the tinkling of toy piano keys. ''He's in the playroom—the big room right off the kitchen.''

She paused a second to kick off her pumps and rooted through the toy-crowded closet for a pair of the knitted slippers she kept for guests. Her regular slippers were packed in her suitcase and there was no time to unpack them.

She'd just eased her cold, pinched toes into the second slipper when a deep groan reached her ears from the playroom.

''Oh, buddy!''

Hope padded down the hall into the kitchen. When she saw the naked toddler and the suspicious network of puddles that streaked her kitchen floor like the

canals of Venice, she sternly told herself that things
could be a lot worse. She could be spending her wedding night with a man who didn't want to be married
to her.

KYLE HOWLED bloody murder when Quinn hauled
him off to the bathroom to clean him up. Quinn gritted his teeth as he taped a diaper in place and tried
to snap Kyle's outfit around the toddler's thrashing
legs. Hope's tidy bathroom looked as if a brigade of
firemen had bathed in it. Kyle had splashed water all
over the floor and smeared soap on the mirror when
Quinn had tried to give him a quick bath in the sink.
Fresh talons of guilt sunk unrelentingly into Quinn's
stomach. Every passing second he spent with Kyle
and Melanie demonstrated how totally incapable he
was of taking care of them properly.

What would he do if Hope said no?

Her attempt to close the door in his face pretty
much expressed her current opinion of him. Somehow he had to change that.

Leaving a couple of the snaps undone, Quinn carried Kyle back into the kitchen and set him down.
Hope had already finished cleaning the floor and was
opening a tin of apple juice at the counter while she
offered Mel fashion advice on the dress-up clothes
his niece was pulling out of a wicker trunk. Kyle
made a beeline for a pile of blocks.

As if she sensed his entrance, Hope turned toward
him, her mouth set in a thin, tight line, her eyes misty
and golden…and full of questions.

And Quinn felt the full jabbing thrust of the intense
physical attraction he'd once had for her all over

again. She hadn't changed much in ten years, he thought, taking in the wild disarray of her dark brown hair streaming over her bare shoulders. She'd removed the jacket of her suit and wore a Rugrats apron over a silky, lace-trimmed camisole top. Her short pink skirt showed off her great legs and the nicely rounded curve of her hips. All that smooth white skin and lace reminded Quinn of a delectable iced cake on a tea tray. Pure, irresistible sweetness.

Her pointed chin and the delicate joy lines fanning those golden eyes and dimpling the corners of her mouth, still made him think she was the most beautiful woman he'd ever laid eyes on. Maybe because his scrutiny was so intense, he noticed the lone white flower clinging to her hair like a snowflake—which reminded him that she'd had flowers in her hair when she'd come to the door. Had she had a date earlier tonight? Quinn frowned. Tom Parrish hadn't mentioned a current boyfriend, the existence of which might put a serious wrench in his plans.

"I'm preparing apple juice and graham crackers for the children," she said, putting an end to the uncomfortable silence that stretched between them. "Do they have any food allergies?"

"Not that I'm aware of." Quinn clenched his fists, feeling awkward as she set the snack on a kid-size picnic table and told Kyle and Melanie they could eat only at the table. What if Hope had a boyfriend? How could he ask her to sacrifice her personal happiness when that had been his excuse for abruptly severing their engagement? He felt like a hypocrite. He shouldn't have come. He never would have thought of seeking her out if Tom hadn't brought up her name. "I'm really sorry to put you to all this trouble."

"It's no trouble. My plans for the evening kind of fell through anyway." Something about her tone of voice told him she was telling him a half truth, but she folded her arms across her chest and changed the subject—to the heart of the matter—with her usual directness. "So, what brings you to my doorstep at nine-thirty at night? You mentioned my brother-in-law sent you?"

Quinn nodded and gestured toward the hallway. "Maybe we could discuss this out of hearing range of the children? I don't know how much they understand, but they've suffered enough trauma in the last thirty-six hours. I don't want to upset them further."

"Of course." Hope was almost afraid to listen. She couldn't imagine Quentin McClure being dead. Hope had always referred to him as Quinn's better half—the younger-by-fourteen minutes, brainy, mild-natured twin. His death had obviously rocked Quinn hard. Quinn's lean, muscled body quivered with tightly reined emotion as they stepped into the hall. It took all her willpower to hold back the urge to touch him. She'd already agreed to listen to him and had let him into her home. Had even let herself look at him again. Not touching him was her last remaining defense to his unexpected invasion. Somehow she felt that if she didn't cross that line, she could survive this encounter with her heart still intact. "What happened to Quent?" she asked softly.

A muscle throbbed in his cheek. "He and his wife Carrie were found shot to death in their home yesterday morning. It was a professional hit, only the hit man mistook Quent for me.''

''Oh my God!''

Hope pressed her hand to her mouth, trying to hold back the nausea that churned in her stomach and clawed up her throat. Her gaze flew instinctively to Kyle and Melanie, who were dribbling cracker crumbs all over the picnic table. Those poor babies! To lose both their parents like that…. A drop of moisture dripped off her chin and she realized she was crying at the senseless injustice of a family being destroyed and children being orphaned…and Quinn walking around with a price on his head and the guilt of his brother and sister-in-law's deaths on his soul.

Quinn.

She flinched as her eyes met the cold bleakness of his gaze. His emotional overload of pain, anger and guilt forcefully struck her like a whiplash to the chest, the whipcord splitting her ribs and curling securely around her heart. Hope swayed and reached out to him, her fingers seeking the iron band of his wrist. A hundred questions formed in her mind. But only one seemed important. ''What can I do to help?''

''Marry me.''

Chapter Two

Hope snatched her fingers from Quinn's arm and stared up at him open-mouthed, not certain she could believe her ears. It was too ludicrous that she could be dumped at the altar by one man and proposed to by another—especially Quinn!—all on the same day, but Quinn's expression was deadly serious.

"I—I beg your pardon?" she whispered.

"You can marry me. Quent and Carrie named me the children's legal guardian in their wills. But if a contract is out on my head, I don't stand much of a chance of being able to fulfill their wishes. I'm a dead man, Hope. I can't hide out with these kids forever. Every day I stay with them I put them in danger." He ran a hand over his haggard face. "The very least I can do for Kyle and Melanie is give them a real mother to take care of them if something happens to me."

She blinked, completely overwhelmed by what he was implying. She didn't bother to conceal her sarcasm. "That's why you came here? You want to marry me just like that to give the kids a mother?"

"Yes." Quinn's hard, slate gaze held hers and

seemed to etch a path into her innermost secret thoughts. As if he knew the hold he'd had over her heart.

Hope wanted to slap him for his audacity, even as she found a kernel of comfort in the knowledge that she was the one he'd come to in his hour of need.

"Surely you don't have to resort to such a drastic measure," she said stiffly. "The RCMP must be investigating, they'll find whoever—"

He cut her off. "I'm not with the RCMP anymore. The Ottawa-Carleton Regional Police are handling the investigation."

Now Hope was thoroughly confused. Quinn had been completely engrossed in his career with the RCMP when she'd met him at a friend's wedding. It had been part of his excuse for breaking their engagement. That along with some nonsense about him not wanting her to be constantly worrying about his safety and waiting for him to come home—an issue that had arisen after his father's sudden death during a reconnaissance mission with the Canadian Forces. "You're not a police officer?"

His mouth stretched in a wry smile. "My business card says I'm a forensic examiner specializing in counterfeits. I decided to take some of the special skills I learned with the RCMP abroad when a friend of mine, Oliver Wells, turned sixty and retired. Oliver offered me a partnership in a forensic analysis and consultation company. Our company specializes in the prevention and detection of counterfeits and forgeries, which is a long-winded way of saying that we determine the authenticity of currency, checks, credit cards, stock certificates, travel documents. Even university diplomas," he added. "We travel all over the world. Today's technology makes it easier for organized crime rings and individuals to commit fraud and most police departments don't have access to the highly specialized skills and training necessary to conduct these types of investigations. The expertise and skills would only be found at the level of the national police forces in Canada and the United States. European countries turn to Interpol. Our clients are law-enforcement agencies, countries, financial institutions, insurance companies and private businesses."

Hope bit down hard on her lower lip. She should have known he'd only left the RCMP because he'd found a broader arena in which to court more danger and excitement. What was that compared to a tame life of raising a family? Like father, like son.

"How does my brother-in-law factor into this?"

"He's my lawyer. He came highly recommended by a friend." Quinn paused. "I didn't realize you were any relation until he suggested he had a sister-in-law who might be willing to take on Kyle and Melanie. He didn't seem to know about our previous relationship so I didn't bother to enlighten him."

Hope closed her eyes and felt the hurt rumble from her voice and burrow deep into her chest. "How flattering that you didn't come up with my name on your own."

He gripped her shoulders and her eyes fluttered open to meet the uncapped honesty glimmering in the depths of his wintry gaze. Her skin grew sensitized to the heat generated by his touch and the roughened tips of his fingers. Longing unfurled in her like a cluster of spring flowers bursting through a patch of winter ice.

"Frankly, it never occurred to me to seek you out," he said brusquely. "I thought by now you'd be married with four kids." She couldn't move, could barely breathe as he gently extracted a baby's breath bud from her hair, holding it between his square-tipped fingers. Her heart lifted and contracted as if stretching after a long dormancy, then commenced to beat at an alarming rate. "Tom told me about your fiancé who died. I'm sorry."

A flush scalded her face. For the life of her she wasn't going to ask what other information Tom might have confided about her personal life. Had her brother-in-law thought she'd just leap at the invitation to be married? To have an instant family? Her knees threatened to buckle, but pride kept them rigidly locked in place. She pressed her lips closed and counted slowly to ten, trying not to think of Quinn living in her house as her husband. "Aren't there any other relatives?"

"No. Carrie was an only child. Her mother died last year and her father is in a nursing home. He's in no shape to take on the responsibility. Unfortunately, there's no one else. My mother died six years ago." He released her and shrugged, the muscles bunching and grinding together beneath his gray sweatshirt. "Given the circumstances, Tom told me that the most expedient thing for me to do from a legal standpoint is to marry and appoint my wife the guardian of the children in my will. As the children's aunt, there's a much greater chance the court will uphold my wishes because you're a relative. I know this sounds a little extreme, but I don't want to take any chances that the kids could end up becoming wards of the Crown.''

This was so absolutely crazy. Hope's brain scrambled to process all the information he was giving her. Tom had been specializing in family law for a number of years. She had no doubt the advice he'd given Quinn was sound, but a part of her felt she must object on the children's behalf. ''Forgive me for sounding so blunt, but how can you be so sure that your brother and his wife were killed in your place?''

''Quent was a scientist and worked for the Museum of Science and Technology. It's not exactly an environment that inspires violence. You knew him. You know what kind of person he was. I deal with people every day who'd like to see me take a trip into the hereafter.''

''How do you know it wasn't a burglary,'' she protested. ''Or just some deranged person—''

He ran his hand through his hair. ''Because the night they were shot, Quent dropped by my office to collect some tickets to a Senators game at the Corel Centre. I believe the hit man was staking out my office and followed him home, thinking he was me. My address isn't listed in the phone book. Neither was Quent's.''

Hope nodded and felt her throat constrict with pain for him, for the children, and for Quent and Carrie, who'd had their lives cut short. ''I'm so sorry. I sympathize with your situation, but I'm not sure that I can marry you.''

''Are you involved with someone?''

Hope nearly choked. *Not as of 7:00 p.m. this evening.* "No, it's not that."

"Then, what is it?"

She lifted her chin. He was dangling her deepest, darkest desire in front of her with all the scruples of a proverbial devil negotiating the price of a soul. One simple *I do* and she'd be a mother and Quinn's wife. "Have you considered that you may not be doing these children any favors by marrying someone when your heart isn't in it?" She held his gaze. "Maybe you're wrong about all this, and one day you'll decide this marriage was a mistake and put these children through the trauma of a divorce." She couldn't bring herself to add *just as he'd thought their engagement was a mistake,* but the words hung in unspoken accusation between them.

His knuckles grazed her jaw. Another touch, another tender, persuasive assault on her senses. His mouth twisted into a lopsided grin that carved a shallow dimple in his left cheek. A very sexy dimple. "Hit men are results-oriented people, Hope, and I'm not willing to take a chance on being wrong. I don't want you to love me. I don't deserve it. But Quent married Carrie for life and I wouldn't dishonor their commitment to each other and what they wanted for their children by offering you less."

Damn him. She took a silent inventory of his rugged profile and the jagged plates of his muscled chest, her conscience rebelling at the idea of some mercenary killer wanting to destroy him. If he managed to survive, and that sounded like a big if, he'd stay married to her out of guilt. For the children's sake. But the thought of exchanging vows with him might destroy her. It had taken her years to get over him.

She darted a glance at Kyle and Melanie and her reluctance to agree to this crazy proposal melted in a rush of compassion. Kyle had abandoned his snack and was industriously hammering a block at the play workbench. Melanie was fast asleep at the picnic table, a graham cracker still clutched in her hand. How on earth was she supposed to resist those two darlings? "*If* I agreed, I'd be putting my life in danger, as well."

"Yes," Quinn stated unequivocally. "But Tom and I, my partner Oliver, and my friend, Gord Swenson, plan to exercise every precaution possible to keep our location under wraps. No phone calls that can be traced or tapped, no record on a computer disk. I'm driving a car that belongs to another friend of Gord's. We don't even want your family to know." He paused, his Adam's apple working in his lean throat. "As soon as the children have bonded with you, I'm going to leave. I have to do whatever I can to help the police determine whoever is responsible for this. I just can't leave the kids immediately—I'm the only familiar face they have at the moment and I have to think of their needs first."

And that, Hope realized, was how they were going to get through this. By thinking of the children and putting Kyle's and Melanie's needs first. She threaded her fingers through his and squeezed. For an instant he seemed surprised by her touch, then his fingers twined tightly with hers in a bond of shared understanding. Tears gathered in her eyes.

But their joined hands, and the tingling warmth

generated by the contact of their palms made her very much aware that marriage had a physical as well as an emotional commitment.

Her cheeks heated. ''Just one more question,'' she said, determined to make things clear right from the beginning. ''Where do you plan on sleeping while you're here?''

''On the couch, Mrs. McClure. Sex is the last thing on my mind, but we might have to get Tom's legal opinion on whether or not the marriage needs to be consummated.''

Hope blushed from her toes to her scalp at the idea of asking her brother-in-law such a question.

''Or maybe not.'' His fingers tightened a notch around hers, protective and familiar. ''Does this mean you'll marry me?''

She tilted her head back to look up at him and gave him a tremulous smile. ''Yes.''

The glow that warmed his eyes created a stirring of response in her belly. Reminded her of a week long ago when being Quinn McClure's fiancée had brought her such happiness and eventually pain.

''Thank you. You won't have to worry about money. I've got savings, investments, a condo and a business I own half of. Not to mention life insurance and the trust fund Quent and Carrie set up for the kids. It should be enough.''

''I'm not worried. I can manage on my own if need be.''

She saw the tension loosen in the planes of his face. ''Carrie would have approved of you. Quent always did.''

Her voice caught in her throat. "I'll love the children like they're my own flesh and blood."

"I know you will."

"Quinn?"

"Yes?"

"I'm afraid."

"I know. Me, too." His arms came around her then, the solid feel of his hard body bittersweet. But Hope nestled her cheek against his breastbone where she could hear the reassuring pound of his heartbeat and hung on tightly. For better or worse. Till death they would part.

SHE'D SAID YES. Relief settled through Quinn as they carried Melanie and Kyle upstairs to the bedrooms that Hope used for the children who occasionally required night care or spent a few days with her when their parents were away on business trips.

Kyle held fast in his arms, Quinn had feelings he'd never expected to have tumble through him as he watched Hope expertly tuck Melanie into a picket-fence bed in a yellow bedroom where butterflies fluttered from one tulip bloom to another on the walls. Observing Hope with Melanie was like being given a glimpse of what could have been. Mel didn't awaken or utter a peep as Hope moved quietly in the room, closing the blinds, switching on a night light on the dresser. Then she rummaged through Melanie's bag.

"Is this all you brought?" she whispered, gesturing at the bag.

Quinn nodded. He only had a small bag for each child. "The kids were whisked out of the house pretty fast. Someone else packed their things. I didn't want to risk returning in case it was under surveillance," he explained quietly as he cradled Kyle's head against his chest. He hoped the toddler would doze off in his arms.

"It doesn't matter. We can buy more clothes and I've got toys and books galore." She gave him a reassuring smile and pulled from the bag a floppy-eared bunny, its brown fur noticeably worn, that she tucked into bed with Melanie.

When she moved to put Mel's clothes in a drawer, Quinn stopped her. "It would be better if you didn't. We may have to leave in a hurry."

Hope looked stricken as the meaning of his words seemed to seep into her. Abandoning the bag, she hovered over the slumbering child and ever-so-gently cupped one of Mel's curls. "Good night, little lamb."

Quinn turned away. At least something good would come of all this. Hope would have the children she deserved, if not the husband. Quinn had no delusions about what kind of father he'd be, given the chance.

Kyle twisted his head to look up at him, his eyes round and hopeful. "Daddy?"

Quinn gritted his teeth and shook his head. Kyle's brow wrinkled in confusion. Hope closed the door to Mel's room and brushed past him, smelling sweet and feminine.

"I put Kyle's things in the cloud bedroom. I thought he'd like the kites." Quinn followed her into a blue bedroom sponge-painted with fluffy clouds and brightly colored kites.

But putting Kyle to bed wasn't as simple as dealing with Mel. After they'd changed him and put him in the crib, he rose to his feet and rattled the bars. "Ma-ma!" Tears glided down his cheeks in rivulets.

Quinn battled his own frayed nerves as he tried to soothe him. Kyle was so agitated his body generated heat like a miniature furnace. "Hey, it's okay, buddy. Lie down. It's time to go to sleep."

"No. I want Mama." Kyle shook his head miserably.

Quinn felt just as miserable. "He was like this last night, too. He cried for almost two hours before he fell asleep."

"That's understandable. He's too young to comprehend that his parents are gone. He's going to need a lot of reassurance and we'll try to stick to his normal bedtime routine as much as possible."

Being forced to confess that he didn't know Kyle's bedtime routine only made Quinn feel worse. How often had he visited his brother since Kyle's birth? A handful of times?

Hope gave him an encouraging smile. "Don't worry, Quinn. We can ask Melanie tomorrow. She'll be able to tell us. Usually it's a combination of a snack, a bath, a story or songs, a snuggle, that kind of thing. Sometimes they sleep with a special toy or a blanket. Children get very attached to their rituals and need them to settle down. Does Kyle have any special toys or a blanket he sleeps with? I didn't find anything in his bag."

Quinn searched his memory as Hope rubbed Kyle's sturdy back. Strange how such an insignificant thing seemed of such importance when their lives were on the line. "I'm not sure. At one point he had a stuffed monkey he called Bobo or Babbu or something like that, but I don't know if he still has it."

Kyle drew a ragged, gulping breath.

"It's okay, we'll improvise."

Quinn watched in gratitude as Hope opened the closet, revealing two rows of stuffed animals. Her face was animated as she told Kyle his crib was a zoo cage and that he could tend three animals in his cage for the night. Kyle's damp blue eyes widened at the selection.

Hope's light-hearted, sunny laugh when Kyle rejected a white snow monkey in favor of a pink pig made Quinn feel less as though the world was closing in around him. When Hope told Kyle to settle his animals down for the night and to be very careful not to step on them, the toddler happily lay down and arranged his animals around him. Hope covered them with a blanket.

"Quinn and I will be back in a few minutes, Kyle. Show your animals how to close their eyes."

At Hope's signal, Quinn tiptoed out of the room with her and held his breath, waiting for Kyle's howl of protest at being left alone to begin. It didn't.

Hope brushed her hands over her hips, a faint rosy hue highlighting her pale complexion. "If you don't mind, I'd like to change out of these clothes. There's a fourth bedroom at the end of the hall for you—just make yourself at home. Maybe we can meet downstairs in a few minutes. I imagine there are some things we need to discuss."

Her apparent nervousness matched his own. "Sure. I'll stow my gear in the room, but I'll be sleeping downstairs as a first line of defense in case we have an intruder. I'll have an alarm system for the house installed tomorrow.''

She opened her mouth as if to argue, but only a long sigh escaped. "Do whatever you think best." Then she turned and walked away.

While Hope changed, Quinn did a perimeter check of the house to ensure all the doors and windows were locked, and made a mental list of locks he felt needed replacing. No one was going to be able to enter this house without making a lot of noise. He'd get Hope a digital cellular phone, too, in the event someone tried to cut the phone lines, and he'd install a dead bolt lock on her bedroom door. He tried to shake off the fear of leaving the kids and Hope unprotected, telling himself they'd be safer the second he left and made himself a visible target.

Hope came downstairs wearing a pale blue terry bathrobe, the prim bodice and rounded collar of a flower-sprigged flannel nightgown visible underneath. Quinn got the message. Hands off. "I checked on Kyle before I came down. He's asleep. So, what do we do first?"

Quinn glanced at his watch. It was 10:47 p.m. He was supposed to call Tom at a particular pub at 11:00. "We call Tom to confirm the arrangements. He thought we could be married Monday. He's booking a ceremony with a nondenominational minister. We just have to show up with a marriage license."

Hope looked at him as if he was crazy, but her voice remained calm and even. She tried not to remember that once upon a time she'd wanted to be married by her father, who was a minister, in the church she'd been raised in. "Fine. You'll need to accompany me to city hall to get the marriage license. They'll need your signature. If we're lucky, we'll be able to get the license without an appointment. Do you have a birth certificate or a passport with you?"

Quinn nodded, feeling awkward again. The fact that she knew what needed to be done to obtain a marriage license reminded him of her deceased fiancé and her lost dreams.

"We'll need to pay the fee in cash. It could take an hour or so to get the license. Do you want to bring the children with us? I have a friend, Jolie, who pinch-hits for me here at the day care when necessary. I could ask her to look after the children."

"I'd rather bring them with us. I don't like letting them out of my sight."

Her golden eyes softened. "Okay. I'll bring lots of distracting toys."

Quinn didn't think Hope needed toys at all. She was a distraction herself. Her voice. Her hair. The soft curves of her body. And especially those eyes.... He reined in his thoughts. He'd be lucky if he lived long enough to say "I do." And his promise to Tom that Hope wouldn't get hurt included never touching her in the way a husband is meant to touch a wife.

It wouldn't be fair to her if he did. She'd already mourned one man she'd intended to marry.

"Will you need Jolie to look after the kids you regularly care for?" Quinn frowned, considering the risks his presence posed to others. Maybe Jolie could look after Hope's day-care kids at her own home until he was gone. It would be safer that way.

Hope dropped her gaze. "Actually, I'm not working next week. It's a short work week leading up to Easter because of Good Friday, and most of my parents have Easter Monday off, too, so they're taking vacation days to give themselves a ten-day break. Which gives me a ten-day break."

Ten days. It should be enough time for the kids to fall in love with Hope. It had only taken an evening for Quinn to fall in love with her.

He tamped down firmly on that last thought. A trip down memory lane wouldn't do either of them much good. He needed to stay focused. "That's one problem solved. I'll make sure I'm gone before you resume operations." Creasing open his wallet, he extracted the piece of paper on which Tom had written the phone number for the pub. Then he punched in the number and passed the phone to Hope. "Ask to speak to Tom and say you're his wife calling."

Hope felt her hand shake as she gripped the phone. The precautions Quinn was taking—his talk of installing an alarm system, keeping the children within his sight and a bag packed for quick flight, and now, the cloak-and-dagger stuff with the phone—only increased her fears.

What if the hit man somehow learned Tom was assisting Quinn? The thought didn't bear thinking about.

Hope heard the sound of a guitar and a smatter of applause in the background as her brother-in-law's whiskey-smooth voice came on the line. "Hi, honey. Did your company arrive?"

"Yes, they're here."

"How are the kids?"

She assured him they were fine. "I'm phoning to tell you that Quinn and I have agreed to be married on Monday. We'll get the license first thing in the morning."

"You're a good person. I just hope you won't get hurt. Our friend strikes me as being a man of his word. I'll do my best to protect your interests. But we'll have to keep this news private. I don't think we should tell your sister or your parents."

"Our friend mentioned that. I understand."

"Good. I'll meet you Monday at one at the minister's house. Our friend has the address."

Hope gestured at Quinn to show her the slip of paper the phone number had been written on. Sure enough, there was an address on it, as well. And thank heavens it wasn't the same renovated church where she'd planned to marry David.

"Fine. I've got it, Tom. We'll be there."

Hope punched the end conversation button and raised her eyes to meet Quinn's steady gaze. Her heart twisted painfully at the thought of how brief he'd implied their marriage could be. Her voice trembled. "It's all set. We're getting married Monday at one."

For the sake of those two precious babies sleeping upstairs, Hope prayed this time she'd actually get to exchange vows with the groom.

Chapter Three

Since toasting their nuptials with champagne hardly seemed appropriate, Hope made a pot of hot coffee. Even though Quinn was obviously exhausted, she had questions, lots of them, and now seemed the best time to ask them. She poured two mugs of coffee and passed one to Quinn, who was seated at the old pine table in her kitchen. "Sorry, there's no milk. You'll have to take it black."

His lean fingers tightened around the handle of the mug. "That's the way I like it."

All he wanted was the caffeine to keep him functioning, Hope thought, noting the exhaustion lining his features. She'd offered him something to eat, but he'd told her he'd eaten a hamburger earlier. She sat down across from him. "Do you really think you might have been followed here?"

"The possibility is slim, but police work taught me you live longer if you prepare for every eventuality. Which reminds me," he opened his wallet and withdrew five one-thousand-dollar bills and several one-hundred-dollar bills and set them in a pile in front of her. "This is for you. I want you to keep it with you on your person. Not in your purse—unless it's one of those pouches that you keep strapped around your waist at all times. And keep some ID with you, too. If we need to leave, you won't be able to use credit cards. We'll each keep a bag packed in the car for ourselves and for the kids with whatever supplies you think we'll need. The bags will go with us wherever we go."

"Okay. I'll do it tonight before I go to bed. I'll stock up on groceries tomorrow and buy the kids some more clothes." Hope started making a mental list of things she should pick up.

"There's one other thing, Hope."

"Mm-hmm?"

"If something goes wrong, if he somehow manages to find his way here, I'm counting on you to get the children safely away. I'm the one he wants, but if he views you as an obstacle or thinks you can ID him, he'll kill you, too. And he wouldn't hesitate to kill the children either."

A chill clambered up Hope's spine and spread into her arms, making her fingers tremble. Coffee spilled over the rim of her mug. Quinn's lean fingers cupped her hands, bolstering her with their warmth and strength. "Get to a safe place. Drive to a police station or a place where there are a lot of people. If you make it to a police station have them contact Detectives Thacker and Beauchamp in the Ottawa-Carleton Regional Police's major crime section. I'll give you their phone numbers to keep with you. You can also call Tom. He'll help you." He gave her fingers another squeeze. "I have no intention of letting this bastard take me down, too, but I'll put up a much better fight if I know you and the children are out of harm's way. Promise me."

"I promise." Relief flickered in his eyes as he removed his hands. Hope sighed, already missing his touch. "But there must be another way to deal with this. I don't understand why we don't all stay in hiding together. Couldn't these police detectives you mentioned put us in some kind of protective custody until they make an arrest?"

"What if they don't make an arrest? We're dealing with a professional killer, not some punk who's likely to make a stupid mistake. I've given the police a list of people who could have hired the hit, but it's only gut feeling, nothing solid. Do you really want to just walk away from your home and your day care, not to mention sever all your ties with your family?"

Not see her family? Hope's throat ached. Her mother had been so disappointed when Hope had told her she wouldn't be home for Easter dinner this year. Hope had made an excuse about visiting a girlfriend in Halifax and had planned to surprise her family by showing up with David and announcing their marriage. She couldn't imagine missing her family's noisy Christmases or her nieces' and nephews' birthday celebrations. "I admit I'd miss my family terribly, but we could find a way to keep in touch with them," she insisted. "I could live anywhere. Work anywhere."

"Well, I can't. I've got a partner and clients who count on me. Cases that I'm currently investigating. Court appearances that need to be made or the bad guys go free. I'm not willing to turn my back on those responsibilities."

"Well, couldn't you continue to do the same thing, but under a different name?"

"Not without major plastic surgery. A select group of people have my level of training and skills. Achieving some form of anonymity or working under another name would be impossible. Besides, we can't live in fear for the rest of our lives."

Hope pushed her mug away, unable to stomach the strong brew any more than she could stomach his line of reasoning. "That's the whole point, Quinn. Your remaining alive. I think you'd do more for the children by being with them than by abandoning them with me. Isn't that what you told me you hated most about your father? That he was always gone? That his career in the military was more important to him than his family?"

His lips stretched thin. "I'm not abandoning them. I'm protecting them. Can you honestly tell me they'll be in any better hands than yours while I'm trying to find the bastard who killed their parents? The hit man will be back. I'm expecting him to track me down like a bloodhound after a wounded fox, and I'll be ready for him, second-guessing his every move. My partner Oliver is already planting video cameras at our office—and making some adjustments to our security system. He's also planting cameras in my condo and at our lab. Though we doubt he'll find the lab. We go to great pains to keep its location hidden. If we're lucky, we'll catch the hit man on tape and be able to identify him. If not, we'll come up with some other way to entrap him—even if I have to stage a funeral to lure him out into the open. He might consider that an irresistible opportunity to take a shot at me."

Appalled, Hope glared at him. "Why on earth would you want to make yourself a target?"

"Because it may be the only feasible way to catch him. I won't take unnecessary risks. You'll have to trust me on that."

Trust him? To do what? Get himself killed? Hope fought the anger that flared in her. Since his plan involved marrying her, she was certain that with her luck, the worst could, and probably would, happen. But she wasn't about to confide to Quinn that he'd not only jinxed her heart, but every relationship she'd had since. "Trust is a two-way street," she reminded him. "If you want me to trust you *again,* then I expect to be fully involved in any decision making that affects our lives as a family. And that includes telling me who you think may have reason to hire someone to kill you. I want to know what we're up against."

Quinn didn't miss her emphasis on the word *again.* He sipped his coffee, grateful for the hot liquid burning a path to his gut and reluctantly admitted to himself that she was right. The more she knew, the more care she'd take to follow his security precautions.

"At the top of my list is an Asian syndicate operating out of Hong Kong. A financial institution hired me in January to investigate some counterfeit credit cards that had circulated over the holidays. Typically, the phony blank credit cards are manufactured in one location, then sold or passed on to another location where they are personalized with stolen names and information. In this case, the cards were being encoded with customer information passed to them from an employee in the bank. It took me a couple of months to pinpoint the employee. The syndicate had coerced him into cooperating by threatening to harm his family. He died violently before we were able to get any names out of him and I could identify the principals and whether they were manufacturing the cards or had purchased them.''

''Violently?''

''Believe me, you don't want to know what they did to him. The syndicate may have figured out I was heading up the investigation and ordered a hit on me.''

Hope's golden eyes were wide with alarm. ''Go on.''

Quinn rolled his shoulders to ease the tension gathering there. Discussing his cases in Hope's cozy kitchen, with its windows and refrigerator covered with the artwork of children, somehow seemed sacrilegious. ''Hugh Simons ranks pretty high on the list, too,'' he continued matter-of-factly. ''Simons is the mastermind behind an organized corporate check-counterfeiting ring that I nailed eight weeks ago. A British Columbia pulp mill hired me to find out who was counterfeiting their corporate checks after a local bank refused to honor any more of their checks— legitimate or otherwise. The pulp mill didn't want to make the situation public out of concern that other banks and businesses would stop honoring their checks, as well. I was able to ascertain that the original check used to make the counterfeit checks had been issued to one secretary—a new employee who claimed she'd been approached in a bar and offered twenty-five hundred dollars for her nine-hundred-dollar paycheck and her employee ID. In order to counterfeit something, you need an original to duplicate. And if you know what to look for when you're examining a counterfeit document, you can always determine the original document that was used in its manufacturing."

"Why would they buy her employee ID?" Hope asked.

"If you're going to pass off counterfeit checks as genuine you need ID to prove you're the person the check is made out to. So they print out X number of checks and corresponding IDs. But Simons was more clever than that. He and his accomplices used the phony ID to open up bank accounts at several different banks. Then they printed up a lot of fake paychecks. On the company's payday, they used ATMs to deposit the fake checks in the accounts they'd set up and then made the maximum cash withdrawal allowed. They netted a hundred thousand dollars in one night. I nicknamed them the Payday Ring.

"Anyway, getting back to the secretary, I had a feeling she might be more involved than she claimed, but I couldn't make any connection until I discovered that several other large companies in different areas of the province had fallen victim to the same scam. When I started digging deeper, I found out that one of the other companies had gone to the police, who'd investigated and gotten as far as determining that the counterfeit checks were copied from a female employee's paycheck—a fairly recent employee who'd quit before the police could question her. The police sent me a picture of the woman. She was the same woman who was employed as a secretary in the pulp mill. She was Simons's girlfriend, Connie Franklin. It turned out there were three other members of the ring, as well. They were all arrested and charged, but the matter hasn't gone to trial yet. The preliminary hearing is in a few weeks.'' Quinn shook his head. ''Simons had more fake IDs than a bar full of underage kids. Boxes full of them.''

''So you think Simons ordered the hit so you won't testify against him?''

''Possibly. He had a lucrative thing going and I blew him out of the water. If Simons wanted me dead, he'd want it done now before I testify at the hearing. Once I've given testimony in a pretrial hearing, my testimony would still stand at the trial if I suddenly departed this earth.''

''Which makes Simons an obvious suspect timing-wise,'' Hope said.

''Timing-wise,'' Quinn agreed. ''But the prison sentences for counterfeiting vary from as little as one year to fourteen years in Canada. It's a paper crime—and nobody really gets too upset when a corporation loses money—except the owners of the corporation. Now, defraud some elderly people or prove the bad guy used documents to lie to the income tax department and he'd be facing stiffer prison sentences and hefty fines. It's just as likely that whoever ordered the hit was motivated by revenge rather than by a need to evade criminal prosecution. Some people don't take kindly to having their reputations damaged and their livelihoods destroyed by the revelation that they're crooks.''

Hope's face was white and disapproving. ''Boy, you keep good company. Asian syndicates, crime rings, hit men. I can hardly wait to hear about these other suspects. What are they—drug dealers?''

Quinn refrained from reminding her that she was the one who'd insisted on knowing details. And now probably wasn't the time to confide that more than one drug courier had contacted his company and fabricated a story designed to have him or Oliver check their traveling documents to see if the alterations done to a stolen passport or a counterfeit passport they'd purchased would pass inspection by customs officials. ''Actually, one is a wealthy doctor in the Dominican Republic, one is the son of one of Canada's wealthiest families, and the other was the secretary of a New England coin-collecting society.''

''What was the doctor doing…counterfeiting prescription forms?''

Quinn didn't miss the caustic bite of her question. This was not the type of conversation Hope would want served up daily around a family meal. But at least she was entering this marriage with her eyes wide open. She wouldn't expect more than he could give. ''Actually, Dr. Chavez had counterfeited the medical diplomas that lined his office walls. Somehow he got his hands on some original diplomas and he fabricated his medical schooling and training. He'd never even been to medical school. There are a lot of phony certificates floating around—especially in undeveloped countries where much of the population is illiterate. The Dominican Republic police asked us to assist them with their investigation after they received a number of complaints from families who'd lost someone under Juan Chavez's care.''

''That's terrible.''

"If that's not bad enough, Chavez has so much money and influence that he's been able to delay the proceedings a number of times. I'm supposed to testify for the prosecution in mid-May. It could be he's angry he'll actually go to trial, and he doesn't like the idea of me explaining to a packed courtroom how he counterfeited those diplomas." Quinn's fingers tightened around the coffee mug. "People will go to extreme measures to save face, which is why I told the police that Ross Linville might bear a grudge against me worth killing over."

"You were involved in that? It was all over the news and in the papers—the fall of the house of Linville. Toronto old money and all those department stores his family owns across the country. I remember it was some big bank-loan scandal. Aren't the police looking for him? He skipped bail or something?"

"That's right. His case was supposed to go to trial on Monday—that's one of the reasons I happened to be in town this week, but he skipped bail and disappeared. The police suspect he's somewhere in the Caribbean, but that could just be a rumor."

"But what does a counterfeit specialist have to do with bank loans?" Hope asked, a frown inching across her forehead.

"Well, his family might have money, but Linville had made some bad investments, and his personal coffers were running dry, so he counterfeited some stock certificates and used them as collateral to obtain a bank loan fraudulently to keep his life-style afloat. The bank got suspicious and hired me to examine the stock certificates to make sure they were genuine.

They weren't. The bank decided to contact the police and go public with the information."

"Maybe Linville disappeared so he could stake out your office," Hope ventured.

"I doubt it. It was a professional job and Linville's the type to pay someone to do his dirty work for him."

"Oh. So what happened with the secretary of the society you mentioned? Does he have a grudge against you, too?"

"I'd say so. Adrian Burkhold was the secretary of a coin-collectors' society and I exposed him for a crook in front of his peers. He'd been making counterfeit rare gold coins and selling them on the market as collectors' items at inflated prices. When the society unknowingly purchased some of the coins, Burkhold suggested they invite an expert to verify their authenticity, hoping I'd point out the flaws in his phony coins so he could correct them."

"And you figured out what he was up to?" Hope asked.

Quinn shrugged. "The coins were too rare—there aren't that many in circulation, which made their authenticity immediately suspect. But then, I have a suspicious mind."

"Obviously. What happened to Burkhold?"

"He was convicted six months ago and sentenced to five years in prison, but he threatened to kill me and I have to take the threat seriously. The police are checking to see who he's communicated with lately."

Hope sat back in her chair. "If that's your short list, I don't think I want to hear the long list."

Quinn gave her a half-hearted grin. "I'm too tired to tell it to you anyway. It would take too long." He most definitely did not want to get into the corrupt government officials he'd unveiled, the ones who'd been providing the criminal element in their countries with information on how to bypass his recommended anti-counterfeiting security measures. Sure, some of them might be mad enough to want him brought down, but none, in his opinion, had the resources to hire a hit man.

He started to rise from the table. "I think we should call it an evening. Kyle doesn't always sleep through the night." Hope didn't react, as if she hadn't heard him. She looked deep in thought. He reached for her coffee mug, intending to put it in the sink.

Hope jumped as if the action had jarred her from her thoughts. "I don't suppose it's possible someone ordered the hit on your brother and his wife on purpose—as a way to hurt you?" she proposed.

Quinn looked at her with renewed admiration. "I hadn't thought of that." The cups clattered as he set them in the sink. He couldn't think of a more brutal form of emotional torture than living with the knowledge that he was to blame for Quent and Carrie's deaths.

A MUFFLED NOISE in the vicinity of the front door awakened Quinn. Senses on full alert, his hand reached instinctively beneath his pillow for the nine-millimeter semiautomatic pistol. Another small thud masked his movements as he rolled off the couch and crept toward the doorway to the parlor in the dark, adrenaline spreading through him in a fluid rush. Was someone trying to get in the front door?

He nearly laughed in relief when he saw the hunched white-flanneled figure lugging something heavy from the closet—except it wasn't funny. He could have blown Hope's head off and landed his butt in jail for God knows how long.

Canada had strict gun-control laws and took a dim view of its citizens firing on burglars—unarmed or otherwise. Quinn was an ex-RCMP officer. He knew better. He'd already violated the terms of his Permit to Transport, which only allowed him to transport the gun in a suitcase to and from a firing range and his home. Transporting the firearm to a new location required a separate permit. And he wasn't authorized to carry it on his person. While such permits existed, they were rarely granted without police documentation, and he didn't have the time or the proof necessary to convince the chief of police to endorse his need for a special carry permit.

Quinn knew he could be charged, fined and spend up to five years in jail if he was caught. The penalty would be even stiffer if he had the misfortune to be caught carrying a restricted firearm in his car without the proper license. A criminal record would completely shred his credibility as an expert witness. He didn't want to explain to a defense counsel why he'd willfully disobeyed the law.

He put the safety on the Glock and tucked it in the arm of the chair out of sight. Then he cleared his throat and said her name.

Hope whirled around with a gasp, and whatever she was carrying dropped to the floor like a bag of cement. "Oh my God, you scared me!" she whispered.

Quinn was glad for the shadows that concealed his expression. "Not half as much as you scared me. If it weren't for the shape of your nightgown, I would have tackled you," he growled, anger at what nearly could have happened making his voice more gruff than he intended. "What are you doing?"

"I forgot something in the closet and I needed it."

"Let me give you a hand."

"No, it's okay. Go back to sleep. I can manage."

Quinn flipped on the light switch. His jaw slackened when he saw the open suitcase at Hope's feet and the lacy array of lingerie that spilled from it like exotic blooms.

Her face went beet red. Quinn wasn't sure who was more embarrassed—him or her.

Hope dropped to her knees and started cramming everything back into the suitcase.

Quinn noticed that a pair of black winter boots and a fleece-lined burgundy anorak were also in the bag, along with a hair dryer and a quilted makeup bag. He knelt beside her and reached for a filmy scrap of turquoise lace, intending to help her. But he blanched when he realized just what part of Hope's body the thin strip of lace was supposed to adorn. Her taste in undergarments had grown more adventurous.

She snatched the thong panties out of his hand. "I was going to go away for a few days, but I changed my mind at the last minute," she stammered.

He wondered why, but it wasn't his place to ask. The contents of the suitcase suggested she'd planned a romantic getaway. Was she still hung up on her dead fiancé? "It's okay, Hope. You don't owe me any explanations. And it isn't as if we've never seen each other in our underwear before."

He enjoyed the quick widening of her eyes as she suddenly seemed to realize that all he was wearing was *his* underwear. Her gaze raked over his torso and centered on his gray cotton boxer shorts. To his annoyance, she started to laugh and waved the turquoise lace. "I suppose I should be grateful you didn't catch me parading around in this."

Quinn was the one who was grateful. Time hadn't dulled his body's ability to respond to her. An image of Hope wearing nothing but that lingerie made him turgid. He could barely hear his own thoughts over the slow pound of his heartbeat. His fingers were clumsy as he fumbled with the suitcase, fastening one of the metal clasps. Coherent speech eluded him. "You're safe from me," he finally managed to say.

"I didn't mean to imply otherwise...." She shook her head and her hair tumbled over her shoulders, dark and wild as a gypsy's.

Quinn stared down at her, tormented by her hair, the pouty softness of her lips and memories of how her body fit so delicately against his. "I know what you meant. Are you having second thoughts?"

She moistened her lips. "No."

The thought that he could kiss her now seeded itself in Quinn's brain. With an inner groan, he positioned the broken suitcase under one arm, shielding her view of the nether parts of his anatomy. "Come on," he said brusquely, wanting to lure her away from the Glock in the parlor. "I'll carry it upstairs for you—the clasp isn't locking properly. Maybe you should use another bag to pack your things in.''

A split-second of hesitation hovered in her eyes, but she followed him without a word.

The door to her room stood open and Quinn set her suitcase on an antique pine chest positioned at the end of her double brass bed. Her bedroom suited her. Fresh and sunny as a spring day. Lavender-sprigged wallpaper covered the walls and the sloping ceiling. Crisp white lace panels tied back with purple and yellow ribbons adorned the windows. A yellow patchwork quilt and a pile of ribbon-trimmed pillows covered the bed.

Quinn quickly backed out of her room. Standing near her bed, half-dressed, with a suitcase full of unmentionable garments within reach was too much temptation—even for a disciplined man like himself. ''Good night, Hope.''

''G'night. Sleep well.''

With a deep sigh, Quinn returned downstairs to the couch. He tucked the semiautomatic beneath his pillow and lay staring at the shadowy patterns on the ceiling, remembering Quent. Remembering Carrie. He didn't think he'd ever sleep well again.

9:02 a.m. Saturday

''I'VE BEEN EXPECTING your fax. Tell me McClure is dead.'' The dry voice rattled over the phone, brooking no argument.

Sweat beaded on Mercy's forehead as he glanced at the photographs in the morning paper. The neighbors had been most uncooperative yesterday. They'd all refused to talk to him; now he knew why. Mc-Clure had a day's head start. "Not yet, but he soon will be." His stellar reputation had not been earned by making mistakes.

"How can this be?"

Mercy pinched the bridge of his nose. He disliked explanations. To him they sounded like excuses for lack of professionalism. "I was not informed the man had an identical twin—with the same initials. It was an unfortunate incident of mistaken identity. But you have my word the situation will be rectified immediately."

"See that it is. And Mercy...make it look like an accident. I don't want a shred of evidence to link the two events."

Chapter Four

Mercy hadn't slept in forty-eight hours. His reputation was on the line. And he hadn't achieved his unprecedented success rate without learning how to accurately assess the risk factor of every move he made. With soundless efficiency, he broke into the reception area of the trendy Bank Street office of McClure & Wells, Document Security Consultants, knowing his time was limited. The alarm system was sophisticated and state of the art, not easily circumvented. He'd grab what he could and examine it later.

The client was getting anxious. The surveillance Mercy had conducted on McClure's brother's house had been a waste of time. McClure hadn't returned. Mercy needed his home address, and he hoped he'd find it here.

Mercy already had an information broker working on a list of calls made from McClure's office line. The Rolodex, appointment book and message pad on the receptionist's desk were the first items to go into the black bag Mercy carried. It took only seconds to defeat the locks on the desk drawers where he found several personal pieces of mail and some photos of school-aged children. There were no diskettes. He checked the wastebasket, but it was empty. Even the wastebasket of the shredder was empty.

Spying the fax machine, he removed the imaging film from the cartridge and dropped that into the bag. That, at least, could be highly informative. Even the most security-conscious people overlooked how revealing the imaging film inside the cartridge of a fax machine could be.

Mercy made short work of the lock barring him admission to McClure's private office. From the surveillance he'd done on the building, he knew McClure's office was on the right. The certificates hanging on the walls confirmed that fact. He rifled the desk and the filing cabinet, annoyed that there were no files or diskettes anywhere. Not even a damn notepad or a scrap of paper that might give him a lead as to where McClure could be hiding out. He figured there had to be a safe somewhere, but he didn't have time to search for it. All he could spare was thirty seconds to search Oliver Wells's office. He might have tripped a silent alarm and he wanted to be long gone before any police arrived.

It proved well worth the risk. What he found brought a smile to his lips.

HOPE WOKE with a start on her wedding day to the tug of little fingers shaking her arm. She opened her eyes, accustomed now to the sheer panic haunting Melanie's expression. After Melanie had wakened her on Saturday morning with the same expression,

Quinn had explained that the preschooler had found her parents and hadn't been able to wake them.

"Good morning, lamb." Hope opened her arms wide, worried about the long-term effects such a discovery could have on her soon-to-be niece. "Have you come for a snuggle?"

Melanie nodded and climbed onto the bed, nesting herself like a kitten against Hope.

Hope held her tightly and prayed that nothing would prevent the wedding from taking place six hours from now—or prevent Quinn from signing his new will naming her as the children's guardian. Even though their future looked bleak, the thought of exchanging vows with Quinn, of being his wife, sent tremors skittering over her limbs like tingling caresses. She just had to believe Quinn would find a way to keep them all safe.

She'd tried hard to shield Kyle and Melanie from the tension of the past two days. She'd read to them, played with them and taken them to the playground at a nearby fast food restaurant to keep them out from underfoot while Quinn supervised the installation of a security alarm—including a panic button resembling a necklace that she wore around her neck. She could press the panic button anytime while she was at home and signal the alarm company. Yesterday, they'd shopped for necessities for the children and a digital cellular phone.

Hope didn't want the children to pick up on her fear, but still, her heart trembled when she heard the slowing of a car engine on the road or when she found Quinn cautiously peering out a window, scanning her property for signs they were being watched.

Kyle had stirred twice last night and Hope had looked out her bedroom window both times before settling back in bed. The creaks and groans of the farmhouse which had once seemed so comforting now sounded like warnings of an intruder.

"Hope," Melanie said in a small voice. "I miss my mommy and my daddy. How come they went to heaven?"

"Because it was their time to go." She smoothed Melanie's hair. "We all go to heaven some day, lamb."

"Won't they ever come back?"

"No sweetheart, I'm afraid not. But they can see you and send you butterfly kisses through the holes in the clouds." Hope lightly tickled Melanie's cheek and was rewarded with a giggle. "So whenever you feel a little brush on your cheek like this, you'll know your mom and dad are sending you a kiss and thinking of you."

Melanie turned her head and slanted a glance up at Hope, her brown eyes uncertain. "Uncle Quinn says I get to be a flower girl today and you're going to be our aunt."

"Yes, lamb. I will love you and Kyle, and I will help Quinn take care of you like your mommy and daddy did. We'll all be a family." At least she hoped so. The thought of Quinn leaving them terrified her. She wanted this marriage to be real. To last.

"Will we live in our house?"

"No, we'll live here in my house for now."

"What about my toys?"

Hope skirted the issue. "We'll see what we can do about having your toys and things sent here."

"When?" Melanie pressed.

"Soon."

"But I want my babies and Kyle misses Blue Baboon."

"I know, lamb." Kyle did indeed miss his Blue Baboon. He'd asked for it umpteen times on Saturday. Melanie had informed Hope that Blue Baboon was her brother's favorite stuffed animal. Kyle had dropped it in the toilet when her daddy was brushing Kyle's teeth and her mommy had said she was going to wash it. Hope figured that whoever had packed the kids' bags hadn't thought to check the dryer for the toy. Kyle had fussed for over an hour last night before falling asleep. The novelty of being a zookeeper had worn off and he'd looked at Hope with sorrowful blue-gray eyes and searched the shelf in the cloud bedroom for his "Bu Baboo." Quinn had taken Melanie to four different toy departments yesterday to scout for a matching baboon without success.

Hope sighed. It seemed terribly unfair that the children were separated from everything familiar to them. With all the precautions Quinn was taking, a side trip to his brother's home for Blue Baboon would be out of the question for the moment. And if the children were this upset about their belongings, Hope wondered what kind of effect Quinn's leaving would have on them.

As if he didn't want to be left out of the discussion, Kyle let out a roar to indicate he was ready to be freed from his crib. Hope reluctantly released Melanie from their cozy snuggle. "There's your brother."

Kyle's bellow turned to a plaintive cry when Hope

opened the door to his room. With an imperative air, he lifted his arms to her. "Down."

She scooped him up and smoothed a rakish wispy curl before kissing him on the forehead. "Not yet, scamp. We've got to change that diaper first."

With Kyle smelling sweetly of talcum powder, the three of them went downstairs a few minutes later. Quinn was in the kitchen cracking eggs into a glass bowl. He'd pulled on a pair of faded jeans and a blue and black plaid shirt hung open over his chest giving her a tantalizing glimpse of dark hair that trailed towards his navel.

Kyle strained toward Quinn, expecting a hug. "Daddy…?"

Quinn's expression tightened as he wiped his hands on a dish towel and patted the toddler's stomach. "Morning, buddy."

Melanie hovered at the entrance to the kitchen and Hope could see the uncertainty on the little girl's face as she gazed at her uncle. "Does it make you mad when Kyle calls you Daddy, Uncle Quinn?" she asked in a voice barely above a whisper.

Out of the mouths of babes, Hope thought, watching as Quinn evaded Kyle's attempts to climb onto him and stepped around the counter to crouch down in front of his niece. "Oh sweetheart, it doesn't make me mad. Kyle's too young to understand about twins looking alike. I may not be your real daddy, but I'll do my best to be as good a daddy to you and Kyle as my brother was."

Melanie's relieved smile made Hope's eyes mist. Hope turned away and asked Kyle if he wanted to watch "Sesame Street" until breakfast was ready, granting Quinn and Melanie some additional privacy.

By the time Quinn rejoined her in the kitchen a few minutes later, Hope had set the table and got the coffee brewing.

"Did I say the right thing to Melanie?" he asked her.

Hope's heart fluttered nervously as their gazes linked. Was he experiencing any pre-wedding jitters, too? Or had he resigned himself to the marriage as being part and parcel of accepting responsibility for his brother's children? "Yes. She was looking for reassurance that you'll be there for them. I think Quent would have been proud of your answer."

Quinn still looked unconvinced. "Yeah, well, we may have been identical twins, but we were different people inside. He was so focused on his family life. He wouldn't play golf with me on Saturday mornings because that was Carrie's day to sleep in and his special time to spend with the kids. He usually took them out for breakfast. He had so much patience. I just don't see myself—" He broke off suddenly.

"—as a devoted husband and father?" Hope finished for him. She popped slices of bread into the toaster to avoid looking at him. Surprisingly the doubts Quinn had unburdened didn't sting. Maybe it was because she'd come to terms with the fact that their dreams weren't in sync long ago. "It's okay," she assured him. "You're only being honest."

In a few hours they'd be married and she was deeply grateful that they at least had honesty and a solid commitment between them, with no false expectations. That was a more solid foundation than some marriages were based on. And she didn't blame Quinn for feeling overwhelmed by the situation. She was feeling overwhelmed herself. The thought that a hit man could be spying on them, even as they spoke, was unnerving.

Quinn fell silent as guilt swelled in him like a thick cloud of smoke. He didn't for a minute believe that he could ever fill his brother's shoes or that Kyle and Melanie would be calling him Daddy a year or two from now. He'd totally destroyed four lives, six if he included his life and Hope's. He'd kidded Quent about not having a security alarm on the house. But they'd thought it an unnecessary expense when Carrie was home with the children all the time. Why hadn't he pressed the point harder?

Hope's voice intruded into his thoughts. "Hey, I think you've beaten the eggs into submission. You've probably pulverized any shells that fell in, too."

He shot her a look meant to quell, but his anger fizzled like air leaking from a balloon when he saw the half-hearted smile on her freshly scrubbed face and the anxiety hovering in her eyes. The belt of her pale blue bathrobe was pulled snug at her waist and her hair was caught up in a butterfly clip. She was standing far too close to him for his own comfort, unloading cutlery from the dishwasher basket into the drawer.

He'd been trying to keep a minimum arm's length distance between them since he'd had an eyeful of her lingerie Friday night. It was much easier to think of her as the children's second mother, rather than as his wife. Or potentially his widow.

She deserved a lot more than he had to offer her.

Today wasn't exactly going to be the big family wedding of her dreams. He knew she'd always wanted her father to officiate at her wedding ceremony. The least he could do was try to make it special for her somehow. Quinn risked closing the gap between them. The fragrant scent of her gently enveloped him and played havoc with his thoughts. He yearned to slip his arms around her waist and pull her close. He cupped her chin instead. "Hope?"

"Yes?"

"You're going to make a beautiful bride today."

She blushed a delicate pink and Quinn felt his chest expand. For a bliss-filled moment, his worries receded and his world narrowed to him and Hope and the ceremony this afternoon—and the fact that he'd get to kiss the bride.

THEY WERE LATE leaving the house. Kyle fussed through breakfast and had thrown most of his scrambled eggs on the floor. When Hope let him out of his high chair, he lay down on the floor and screamed for his Blue Baboon. Quinn tried to comfort him, while Hope hurriedly did the dishes and prepared snacks and juice for the diaper bag.

It took forever to get everyone dressed and into the car. Telling herself she wasn't being superstitious, Hope had decided not to wear a dress. But when Melanie came into her room and saw her in black wool slacks, a dusty rose silk blouse and a black-and-white houndstooth check blazer and insisted that Hope couldn't be a bride unless she wore a pretty, white dress, Hope pulled from her closet a white batiste tea-length gown her mother had given her for her birthday last July. It was hopelessly Edwardian in styling, with pearl buttons, satin trim and lacy frills. The type of dress she'd once loved to wear on hot summer days when she'd believed in romance and fairy tales, and the thought of Quinn undoing all those buttons made her smile in anticipation. Hope had worn the dress to a lunch date with her mother and sisters, then had hidden it in the back of her closet.

Hope wore the pearl earrings that her parents had given her for her sixteenth birthday and dabbed on a bit of perfume. Melanie, of course, wanted to wear perfume, too.

Hope obliged her and took a few minutes to comb out Melanie's curls. She looked adorable in a lavender dress dotted with tulips and yellow duck-lings.

Taking a last uncertain look at herself in the mirror, Hope grabbed a soft shell-pink wool blazer to tone down the dress and hustled Melanie downstairs. What would Quinn think when he saw her?

To her disappointment, he didn't say anything. His eyes had that impenetrable granite cast to them that made her wonder what private thoughts were lurking behind them. He didn't have a suit to wear to the ceremony, but she thought he looked heart-trippingly handsome in gray corduroys and a loose-fitting black wool sweater. Hope put her winter coat on, hiding the dress.

They had been on the road ten minutes when she heard the strange pop.

"Quinn—what's happening?" she cried out, a bolt of fear shooting from her heart to her soul as the car swerved crazily on the isolated country road, heading for a snow-filled ditch.

"Get your head down and stay down."

She obeyed instantly. *Oh my God. Had they been shot at?*

The car jerked to a halt. Before Hope knew what was happening, Quinn was out of the car, slamming the door behind him. Hope couldn't see what he was doing, but she noticed he'd locked the driver's side door. Kyle started to whine. "It's okay, sweetie, he'll be right back." Hope prayed that was the truth as she dug into her purse for the cellular phone Quinn had bought her.

Seconds later, she heard a tap on her door. Hope raised her head and saw Quinn through the window. Her bones turned to rubber in weak relief when he mouthed, "False alarm."

She rolled down the window, struggling to keep herself from reaching out to touch him. She didn't want him to know how scared she'd been. A cold wind whipped into the car.

Quinn looked wary, his vigilant gaze darting past her to scan the roadway and the open fields. "We've got a flat. The tire's pretty worn." Which she interpreted to mean the tire hadn't burst because they'd been shot at. "Pass me the keys so I can get the spare out of the back. You'll all have to get out of the car while I change the tire."

The morning went from bad to worse when Quinn discovered the spare tire had no air. Hope couldn't help but feel that the flat tire was a bad omen as Quinn called a tow truck.

The tow truck arrived twenty-five minutes later

and transported them to a service center where Quinn had two of the tires and the spare replaced. Their luck didn't improve once they arrived at city hall. They didn't have an appointment to obtain their marriage license and there was a line. Neither of the children were interested in the toys and picture books Hope had brought. Kyle whined and clung to Quinn's leg, while Melanie complained she was thirsty and wanted juice.

Hope managed to satisfy Melanie with a carton of apple juice and a story about fairies, but she was worried about Kyle. His forehead felt suspiciously warm, but then, the waiting room was stuffy. Was his obvious misery his way of acting out his grief? Or was he coming down with something?

It was almost noon by the time they'd filled out the forms and were granted a marriage license. Once they got to the car, Hope removed the digital thermometer from the first-aid kit she'd packed and took Kyle's temperature. He had a fever.

Getting him to take a dropperful of fever relief medicine took all of her ingenuity. Melanie told her it wasn't the same medicine their mommy used.

"Is he going to be okay?" Quinn asked, sliding behind the steering wheel. The rigid, controlled movement of his limbs suggested his nerves were as frayed as hers about their upcoming nuptials.

Hope gave him the most optimistic smile she could manage considering her stomach felt as if it was filled with swarming bees. Anything and everything seemed to go wrong whenever she decided to get married, why should today be any different? "Kids get fevers all the time," she assured him. "He's probably teething. After the wedding, we'll pick up some of the pain reliever he's used to taking.''

But her fingers shook as she snapped her seat belt on and Quinn started the engine. They barely had time to grab some lunch and make the half-hour drive to the wedding ceremony. Still, Hope knew it was plenty of time for something else to go terribly wrong.

Chapter Five

Satin. Hope's lips felt like sun-warmed satin and her mouth tasted of honey and spice. Quinn forgot that Kyle's knees were clamped mercilessly around his hip. He forgot about Melanie who was sprinkling silk daisies and red confetti hearts from a white wicker basket onto the Persian carpet at their feet. He forgot about the chaplain and Tom and the paralegal, and simply lost himself in the tentative sweetness of Hope's kiss.

It was everything he'd feared and more. And never to be repeated. But he wouldn't deny her this symbolic kiss—just as he couldn't deny her the ring he'd bought for her yesterday.

Quinn was rudely returned to reality by a tiny right hook landing on his cheek. "No!" Kyle said sharply.

They broke apart laughing. The pale blush of color warming Hope's cheeks and the golden sparks flaring in her eyes told him he'd done something right. The Victorian parlor the gregarious chaplain used for wedding services wasn't the same as being married in a church, but it was warm and intimate.

Quinn bent down to appease the flower girl who was demanding a kiss.

Then matters turned more solemn as the Reverend Drake invited them over to an elegant mahogany table to sign their marriage certificate. Tom and his paralegal, a round-faced woman with a nervous laugh, added their signatures as witnesses. Then the chaplain and the paralegal witnessed the signing of Quinn's will.

Quinn felt enormously relieved once his will was signed. He clasped the lawyer's hand. "Thanks, Tom."

"Stay safe." Tom said meaningfully. "I'll get word to Oliver through Gordon that the ceremony went off without a hitch and I'll pass him Hope's new cell phone number so he can reach you in an emergency. I'd like a private word with Hope before you go."

Because Kyle was so irritable, Quinn hustled the kids into the foyer to put on their jackets while Hope spoke to Tom in the parlor. Quinn was no expert, but even *he* could tell that Kyle's fever was rising.

Melanie tripped in the parking lot, scattering daisies and red confetti hearts from her basket into the mud. Quinn did his best to soothe her as he gathered the daisies that weren't too badly soiled. But the basket and Melanie's face and clothes were a mess. He wiped them down with baby wipes from the diaper bag and was bundling the kids into their car seats when Hope returned to the car. He didn't know what she'd talked to Tom about, but judging by the tight press of her lips, she was upset. She wouldn't meet his gaze.

"Everything okay?" he asked quietly as he put the key in the ignition.

"Yes. Tom had some questions about you. He's worried about me." She didn't elaborate. Quinn let it go.

He knew she was lying anyway.

WEDDINGS OF YESTERYEAR. The Reverend Edward T. Drake, wedding chaplain. The address on the bottom of the fancy scrolled sign matched the address written on a yellow sticky-note Mercy had found in Quinn McClure's file in the lawyer's office not more than an hour ago. Mercy slowed the car and craned his neck to see as he drove past two brick posts fronting the entrance to a drive that curved toward an old redbrick house with a gable popping up in the center of its metal roof and a porch dripping with gingerbread trim. Mercy spotted a parking lot to one side of the house. The damn parking lot was empty. After everything he'd gone through to gain access to McClure's lawyer's office this morning, he'd missed them!

Swearing again, Mercy continued down the two-lane highway for another kilometer before making a U-turn and doubling back. He'd have to go inside. There hadn't been time to change clothes after he'd set the fire in Parrish's building and his clothes reeked of smoke. When he turned into the drive he saw that there was another house on the property set back beyond a screen of evergreens. It was a modern rancher with an attached garage. Presumably the private home of the minister. Mercy parked in a corner of the muddy gravel lot where his car wouldn't likely be as visible from the road or the other house and climbed onto the porch. A light burned in the front hall. Mercy tried the door. It was unlocked.

"Hello," he called out, carefully wiping the mud from his feet before he stepped into a dark-paneled foyer. A grandfather clock near the stairs told him it was 1:42. "Anyone here?"

"Coming," a reedy voice replied from somewhere toward the back of the house. An elderly man with hunched shoulders and eyes like black stones, emerged from a room and approached with a wide smile. "Sorry to keep you waiting."

"Am I too late for the McClure wedding?"

"'Fraid so. They left about five minutes ago. I'm finishing up the paperwork now. It was a lovely ceremony."

Mercy listened carefully for sounds that might indicate someone else could still be in the house. "I'm the bride's brother from out-of-town. There was supposed to be a lunch afterward. You wouldn't happen to know where?"

The minister frowned. "Sorry, no one mentioned it, though they seemed in a bit of a hurry. The baby wasn't feeling well. Wish I could be more help."

Mercy smiled as he reached for his piece. "I'm sure you will be." He shot the old man in the forehead before the surprise could register in Edward T. Drake's eyes.

Not wanting the police to connect this consequential act with the McClure hit, Mercy put on a pair of gloves and divested the man of his wallet and watch so the police would think a robbery had taken place, then strode down the hall to the room where the minister had been doing his paperwork.

It didn't take long to help himself to the contents of the cash box hidden in the lower desk drawer and find Quinn McClure's home address as well as the name and address of his bride. Now he could close in for the kill.

THEY WERE actually married. Hope clenched the plastic bag from the pharmacy tightly in her lap and stared in disbelief at the simple gold band circling the ring finger of her left hand as Quinn sped through traffic on Hazeldean Road. The drive back to Kanata had finally knocked out both Kyle and Melanie. Every now and then, Hope heard a gentle snore or a deep sigh from the back seat. She felt more like a limp rag than an exultant bride. The day had been exhausting, and Quinn's kiss had only added to the trauma.

It was hard enough to be his wife in name only in the face of a desperately uncertain future, without being physically reminded of how thoroughly persuasive his kisses could be. He'd been her first lover all those years ago. From the moment they'd met, she'd resisted his takeover of her heart, finding excuses to throw in the way of the heady, out-of-control feelings that made her want to be closer to him than she'd ever been to another man. Quinn's kisses had melted her defenses then, and Hope feared they were equally as potent now. Tom's suspicions had certainly been aroused. Hope had thought that telling him about her brief engagement to Quinn would allay

Tom's concerns. On the contrary, it had had the opposite effect.

Tom wanted to know why Quinn hadn't mentioned their engagement when her name came up in the conversation.

Hope had stopped his questions with a grateful hug. "You might think he owes you an explanation, but he doesn't. The only explanations he owes are to me. I'm just glad he came to you for help."

Tom had hugged her back. "I don't want you to get hurt."

Hope didn't want to get hurt again either. The love she'd had for Quinn wasn't gone, only resurrected. She glanced at Quinn's strong profile beneath her lowered lashes as he turned the car onto March Road. Suddenly, inexplicably, her innermost wish had been granted and she felt as if an evil genie was taunting her from the sidelines to be careful what she wished for. Quinn was her husband now. Losing him would be unbearable. But the prospect of spending a life together knowing he felt trapped into the marriage made her stomach tighten.

Quinn's voice, low and urgent, pulled her sharply from her thoughts. The car was slowing. "There's a car parked down the road past your driveway."

"Where?" she asked, scanning the road ahead. The houses were farther apart on this stretch of March Road. Some of her neighbors farmed or boarded horses, others just enjoyed the acres of privacy.

"Tucked into the thicket of birch trees."

Hope saw it now. A darker metallic blue.

"Have you ever seen anyone parked there before?"

"No. Maybe someone's having car trouble."

Quinn pulled over and put the car in park, leaving the engine idling. "Maybe. I'm going up to the house to check it out. Better safe than sorry. Get in the driver's seat. If I'm not back in five minutes, get the children someplace safe like we discussed."

The unease that had crimped her spine all day erupted into a violent spasm of panic. She gripped his arm, feeling the bunched knot of his biceps. The possibility that Quinn wouldn't live beyond their wedding day seemed chillingly real. "No. Don't. We'll just go away somewhere—the four of us."

He twisted toward her, his eyes glittering like shards of glass and his mouth grim. "We don't have time for a discussion. I know you're scared, but I'm counting on you—"

She cut him off. "But you don't understand..." she faltered, searching for the words to explain the jinx that had tainted her life whenever the merest hint of matrimony surfaced.

"What I understand, Hope, is that two people are already dead and we are not going to live in fear for the rest of our lives."

Kyle muttered in his sleep and Hope instinctively glanced into the back seat to check on him. Melanie was still napping, too. Oh God, much as she hated to admit it, Quinn was right. These children couldn't go through life with fear dodging their heels. She released her grip on Quinn's arm.

"Don't slam the car doors," he warned as he eased

his own door open. "We don't want to give him any advance warning of our arrival."

Hope's heart pounded like a bomb set to explode as she climbed into the driver's seat and watched Quinn cut through the field and jump the white rail fence that bordered her yard. Then he disappeared behind a bank of pine trees and fear jammed in her throat.

Quinn forced all thoughts of Hope and the children from his mind and focused on the task at hand. Over the weekend, he'd familiarized himself with Hope's property. As soon as he was out of her view, he drew his gun. He approached the house with caution, shielding himself behind trees and shrubbery, alert for the slightest sound or movement. The fact that the security company hadn't called to say there had been an intruder told him the hit man was most likely outside, hidden in the brush, anticipating a clear shot when he pulled up in the driveway.

Quinn pressed his back to the east wall of the house and risked a look around the corner. His breath froze in his lungs when he saw a husky man in an olive-green coat and tan slacks on the porch, peering into Hope's living-room window.

Quinn went in for the kill.

HOPE DIDN'T WANT to think about what could be happening up at the house. Her gaze flew back to the car wedged into the trees down the road. Suddenly, it occurred to her that it might help if she could obtain a description and license plate number of the car. Surely there would be no harm in driving past it. She could turn around in the Markhams' driveway. Hope put the car in gear and pulled back onto the road.

It took all her willpower not to brake suddenly as she drove past the thicket. She couldn't make out the license plate, but Hope recognized the vehicle's make and the advertisement for David's accounting firm painted on the side of the sedan. Her blood ran cold. What on earth was her ex-fiancé doing here?

Oh God, what if Quinn hurt David? Or killed him? Hope braked hard, checked her rearview mirror to make sure no cars were behind her, then made a U-turn in the middle of the road. Her arms trembled as she pulled into the driveway. Gravel spewed out beneath the tires as she sped up the lane, pressing on the horn.

Kyle awoke with a cry, startled by the noise.

"Hope? Are we home?" Melanie murmured sleepily.

"It's okay, kids, I just felt like making some noise," Hope said with false cheeriness. Her stomach plunged in horror as she brought the car to a halt in the parking area, and her gaze landed on the two figures locked in combat on the porch. Quinn was straddling David's prostrate form, his fist raised to deliver a blow.

Hope leapt out of the car, shrieking as she ran up the brick path. "No! Quinn, stop! He's a friend of mine."

Hope nearly fainted when she saw the fury in Quinn's eyes and the blood covering David's face. She pushed at Quinn's shoulders. "Get off him. Oh God, David, are you all right?"

David groaned and rolled into a fetal position, his

hand fumbling in the pocket of his jacket for a hand-kerchief. "I think he broke my nose. Who is this crazy bastard?"

"Who the hell are you?" Quinn demanded. "And what were you doing peeking in Hope's windows?"

Hope blanched. David had been peeking in her windows? She turned to Quinn, pleading him with her eyes. "Quinn, I can handle this. Please go get the kids out of the car."

"I'm not leaving until I find out who this jerk is. Is that your car parked down by the road?"

"What of it?" David said with belligerence in his tone, pushing himself upright. His dark brown eyes blazed with outrage. "I'm Hope's fiancé. I'll park my car wherever I damn well please."

"Her fiancé? That's funny. I'm her husband."

"Her what?" David's jaw dropped. Hope wished the floorboards would splinter open and swallow her whole. "Since when?"

Quinn's face was a granite mask. "Since about one o'clock this afternoon."

"You're married to this bastard?" David struggled to his feet, and Hope reached out to help him. Blood had dribbled onto his coat and she could see some angry swelling around his right eye and along his jaw.

"It's not what you think," she began, then realized she didn't owe David any explanations. And she didn't particularly want to have this conversation with Quinn as an interested audience either. "Quinn, please get my purse from the car. My keys are inside it. David's going to need some ice and some ban-dages."

Quinn didn't budge. He hovered over David like he didn't give a damn about first aid.

David gave a strangled laugh. "Don't bother, I'm leaving. I came here to apologize for letting Susan ruin our wedding and to ask you to forgive me, but I guess my timing's a little off."

Hope gripped his arm when he swayed. "You didn't marry Susan?"

"No. I've been such an idiot, Hope...."

Hope suddenly realized that Quinn was still blatantly listening to their every word. She whirled around, anger making her tone harsh. "I'm going to walk David to his car. Take the children into the house, please. Give Kyle some juice. We don't want him to get dehydrated. I'll be back in a few minutes."

"Fine," Quinn said, brushing past her.

Hope's knees trembled as she walked with David down the drive. She knew Quinn was angry she hadn't told him about David, but she was the one who'd been thoroughly stripped of her pride.

"What don't I understand, Hope?" David asked her once they were well out of Quinn's hearing distance.

Hope was tempted to tell him, but shook her head. "It doesn't matter now. I did get married this afternoon, but I would appreciate it if you didn't make that information public knowledge just yet."

"Why not?"

"Because we're going to throw a party and surprise our families with the news."

"I see." David paused, still holding his handkerchief to his nose. Hope was relieved that the bleeding seemed to have stopped. "I'm sorry I dropped by unannounced. I tried calling this morning and left several messages. Then I drove by and saw your car. I thought you wouldn't answer the door if you saw my car, and I really wanted to talk to you about what happened with Susan.''

''I don't want to talk about Susan.''

David had the grace to look embarrassed. He smoothed down his dark hair. ''Okay. We won't talk about Susan. I never wanted to hurt you.''

''I know.''

''So, how long have you known this guy? You never mentioned anyone named Quinn.''

True enough. Past relationships were a sensitive subject she preferred to keep to herself, though she had told David about Matthew and his tragic car accident. Hope gazed up at David. He was handsome and successful and had some wonderful qualities. But he still had some unresolved emotional issues regarding Susan, just as she did about Quinn. ''I've known him long enough to know I made the right decision,'' she said firmly.

''You're in love with him?''

''Yes.'' The answer came more easily than she expected.

''Then I guess I can forgive him for mistaking me for a Peeping Tom and using my face as a punching bag.''

Hope stopped at the end of the drive. There was no point in walking him any farther. ''Goodbye, David.''

Her body's lukewarm reaction to his kiss on her cheek told her David had made the right decision for both of them when he'd called off their elopement.

With a heavy sigh, she turned back to the house. Somehow she suspected Quinn wouldn't be waiting to carry her over the threshold.

QUINN'S RELIEF that their safe house was still secure was quickly usurped by a disturbing thought that rampaged in his mind like a wild bull on the loose: Hope had married him on the rebound. Now he understood those little white flowers in her hair and the sexy lingerie in her suitcase. She'd obviously planned to elope with David on Friday. Had David dumped her for someone named Susan?

Quinn exhaled an exasperated breath, knowing his own actions weren't above reproach when it came to his relationship with Hope. He'd known when he'd slept with her that very first time that she'd been saving herself for marriage. And he'd broken a promise to marry her.

Quinn kept an eye on the clock as he encouraged Kyle to sip from a small cup filled with apple juice. His nap in the car had only made him grumpier. How long did it take to walk half a kilometer anyway? And why hadn't Hope breathed a word about her engagement when he'd asked her if there was someone special in her life?

Quinn winced as Melanie banged a plastic pot on the toy kitchen and sang a nonsense song about sandwiches. Part of him wondered how Quent and Carrie had managed to have a rational thought, much less a rational conversation, with these two underfoot.

Why hadn't Hope told him the truth?

Instead, she'd let him dump his problems in her lap because she had a heart bigger than the province of Ontario when it came to children. Now her fiancé was begging her forgiveness, and Quinn was painfully aware that their marriage was preventing her from reconciling with David.

Guilt speared him. He'd shattered her dreams of a home and family not once, but twice.

His heartbeat ground to a halt when he heard the door open.

"Quinn?" she called out.

His throat had never felt more dry. What if she'd decided to go back to David? "In the family room."

The telltale smear of blood on her chin near her mouth glued him to the seat of the rocking chair where he was trying to comfort Kyle. She didn't look him in the eye, instead, she bent down to retrieve the rainbow afghan, which Kyle had kicked onto the rug a few minutes earlier. "I guess you got an earful."

"I should have let you speak privately."

Her lips pressed tightly together. She dropped to her knees in front of him and crooned at Kyle as she felt his forehead with the back of her hand.

"Kyle, you're a hot potato." Quinn knew she was purposely ignoring him. "Do you know what we do with hot potatoes? We put them in the bathtub with bubbles and make mushy mashed potatoes." The effort she was making for Kyle when she was obviously very upset herself only made his admiration for her sink deeper into his soul—and made him angry. He couldn't afford to harbor those kind of feelings for her again. He wasn't any closer to finding out who had hired the hit man, though his partner Oliver was working on it.

Quinn caught Hope's wrist, accidentally spilling

some of the juice from Kyle's cup. "Don't you know how risky it was to come charging up the driveway with the kids in the car? What if it hadn't been your fiancé? We wouldn't be having this conversation."

Her eyes glittered like yellow diamonds as she met his gaze squarely. "I recognized his car, and I was afraid you'd hurt him. It was a good thing I arrived before you broke more than his nose. You'll be happy to know he won't be pressing charges."

Kyle interrupted with a demand for another sip of juice. Quinn scowled and struggled to keep his tone reasonable so Kyle wouldn't be alarmed. "He was trespassing! That's beside the point anyway."

Hope arched a brow. "And just what is the point?"

"You didn't stay put like I told you. I don't want you taking any unnecessary risks—"

"Like our marriage isn't a risk?"

She was right. And their marriage was keeping her from being with the man she loved. Quinn wondered if she planned to raise Kyle and Melanie with David in the future. Was it any of his business if she did? "I'm sorry about what happened between you and David."

"You're sorry?" She laughed dryly. "David didn't break my heart, Quinn. You have that very special honor."

Her candor shredded his conscience to ribbons. Somehow in his certainty that he was doing the right thing, he'd convinced himself that Hope would forgive him for breaking his promise to her. Now he realized she hadn't, and she probably never would.

And yet, she'd married him anyway because she couldn't turn her back on the children.

His eyes traced her pale features, her determined chin; lingered on the soft mouth that spoke more truth than he was man enough to hear, on her lips that had felt like warm satin and had offered him solace and passion in the midst of the chaos going on around them. He was tempted to tell her he was damned glad she hadn't married David on Friday. And his reasons had nothing to do with Kyle and Melanie.

But even that selfish acknowledgment inspired more razor-edged guilt. The last thing he wanted to do was make more promises to Hope that he couldn't keep. The sooner he left, the better.

Hope jerked her wrist free of his grasp and scooped Kyle up from his lap. "Come on, hot potato, it's time to put you in the big pot."

Anxiety rose in Kyle's glassy eyes as he peered down at Quinn. "Daddy come?"

Quinn couldn't resist Kyle's plea, even though he was sure Hope wouldn't welcome his company in the small confines of the bathroom. "Sure, buddy."

Kyle didn't appreciate a lukewarm bath and he let the whole household know it. But the bath brought his temperature down out of the danger range, though the stress of caring for him only added to the friction Quinn felt gathering between him and Hope like static electricity.

Kyle sat on Quinn's lap during supper and whined for his mommy and his Blue Baboon until Quinn's ears started to ring. Afterward, Hope took Kyle's temperature and gave him another dose of medicine and Quinn discovered how endless an evening could feel when you were pacing a floor, trying to lull a cranky kid to sleep. Melanie, as if sensing Kyle was getting special treatment, invented all kinds of delaying tactics to postpone going to bed. She'd even demanded Quinn kiss her good-night and read her two stories because Kyle got two stories.

Quinn felt the walls closing in around him. He needed to get out for a while. Find a pay phone so he could touch base with Gord and Oliver. See if anything had turned up in the investigation.

Upstairs, Hope thanked the emergency room nurse at the children's hospital for her advice and hung up the phone with a sigh. At least the nurse didn't think there was an urgent need to bring Kyle to the emergency room tonight.

Hope rose and stretched the tired muscles in her back.

A magical, romantic wedding day this was not, but she wouldn't trade it for the world, even though she and Quinn had argued. Denying that she loved him and that he'd hurt her seemed an exercise in futility. His kiss earlier had proved, in a way words could not, that he still desired her.

When she went out into the hall, Quinn was coming up the stairs with Kyle's head drooped on his shoulder. Her heart melted at the sight. There might be hope for a future for them yet.

"I think he's asleep," he whispered.

Hope nodded and led the way into Kyle's room where she lowered the lights and turned back the blankets in the crib.

She held her breath as Quinn eased Kyle off his shoulder and laid him on the mattress. Kyle stirred with a wail and pawed through the blankets. "Bu Babu?" When he didn't find his toy, he rose onto his knees, his face still pressed into the mattress and his bum in the air. A sob shook his little body.

Quinn cursed. Hope felt like sobbing herself. Kyle was just too young to understand all this. She grabbed Quinn's hand and laid it on Kyle's back, hoping Quinn's touch would reassure Kyle he was not completely alone. After a few minutes, Kyle's sobs slowed and he drifted into sleep.

They tiptoed out into the hall, easing the door shut. Quinn sagged against the wall in the hallway, looking discouraged. Even discouraged, he was far too sexy for Hope's peace of mind.

"Quiet at last," he sighed. "Armed felons are easier to put down. Do you think he's out for the night?"

She gestured for him to follow her downstairs so their voices wouldn't disturb Kyle. "Your guess is as good as mine," she said when they had descended to the main floor. "It's hard to tell whether he's teething or just coming down with a virus. If he still has a fever in the morning, we could take him to the clinic in town. Part of his misery could be that he's missing his parents."

Quinn rubbed a hand across his face and grimaced. "Don't forget Blue Baboon."

Hope's jaw trembled. "Well, he doesn't need his Blue Baboon when he has you. Don't you see that? You were great with him today."

"But he isn't always going to have me, Hope. Do you want every day to be like today—being frightened out of our wits over flat tires and guests who drop by unexpectedly?"

"No, I don't want that. But I don't like your solution either. Kyle and Melanie are separated from their parents and everything that's familiar to them and you want to add to their loss by turning yourself into a target. That doesn't make a heck of a lot of sense to me."

"Hit men have their own brand of logic. They get paid to kill and they don't care who or how many, as long as they get their fee. I'm leaving as soon as Kyle's feeling better. But just to show you I'm not a completely insensitive human being, I'm going over to Quent's house to get Blue Baboon." He opened the hall closet and pulled out his jacket, jamming his arms into the sleeves.

"You mean, now?" Fear spiraled through Hope. "I thought you said it wasn't safe to go back to the house. We'll find Kyle another Blue Baboon somewhere—"

"And it wouldn't be any more genuine than I am, passing myself off as his counterfeit dad."

Hope opened her mouth to argue, then snapped it shut. How was she supposed to stop a man with a death wish?

She could only think of one way. Grabbing the lapels of his jacket collar, she felt the stiff resistance of his body radiate toward her like an impenetrable force field as she rose on her tiptoes and kissed him hard. On the mouth.

She'd never felt so scared of being rejected. Her heart hammered with uncertainty. Desire exploded in her as his lips parted. Hope swayed, her breasts brushing his chest, her hips yearning to cradle his as they once had. Her hands slid down the unrelenting planes of his chest, spreading over his ribs to his back in an effort to pull him closer.

Quinn suddenly tore his lips from hers and wheeled toward the door as if she were an evil temptress. "Don't wait up," he said in a strangled voice as he jerked the door open. The door slammed behind him loud enough to wake the children.

Hope leaned against the door, every cell in her body stimulated and left wanting by the oh-so-brief contact with Quinn. The taste of him still lingered on her lips as she listened to the sport utility vehicle's engine turn over, then progressively grow fainter as the vehicle turned out of her driveway onto March Road.

She was alone again on her wedding night.

Chapter Six

Hope prowled the house, tidying up the toys in the family room and calculating just how long it would take Quinn to drive to Gloucester and back. There shouldn't be too much traffic on the Queensway unless there was a hockey game or a special event on at the Corel Centre.

She put the kettle on to boil and told herself that even with traffic delays he should be gone two hours at the most. She wouldn't even let herself worry until eleven. If Quinn wasn't back by eleven-thirty, she'd call Tom.

Her phone rang just as the kettle started to whistle. Hope nearly jumped out of her skin. Her clients and her family knew she was away on holiday. Who could be calling? Quinn?

She reached for the receiver, hoping to hear Quinn's voice. "Hello?"

"Good evening," a man responded in a well-modulated voice. For a second she thought it was a phone solicitation call, until the man addressed her by name, "Am I speaking to Hope Fancy-McClure?"

The skin prickled on the back of her neck as

alarms and bells went off in her brain. "I'm sorry, you must have the wrong number. There's no one by the name of McClure at this residence."

"This is Oliver Wells, Hope. I'm Quinn's partner. It's urgent that I speak with him. We've had a break-in at the office and we have our friend on tape."

Hope hesitated, not knowing what to do. "I'm afraid I don't know what you're talking about," she said cautiously. At the wedding Quinn had given Tom her cellular number to pass to Oliver for just such emergencies. Why hadn't Oliver called her on her cell phone? Had Tom not had time to pass the number to Gordon Swenson who was acting as the middle man between all three men? "My name is Hope Fancy," she said again. "But I really don't have a clue as to what you're talking about. Who gave you this number?"

"Gord Swenson."

That sounded right at least.

"I am Quinn's partner," he assured her. "You're the minister's daughter with the fanciful name. Quinn carries a picture of you in his wallet that was taken the day you met. You met at an evening wedding cruise on the Ottawa River. You were wearing a peach dress and Quinn told me he'd been engaged to you for a short time—his one and only near brush with commitment."

Hope didn't know what to say. Could Quinn possibly be carrying a photo of her in his wallet? Or was this some kind of trick? She *had* worn a peach dress to the wedding.

"I'm sorry—" she began.

"Please don't hang up, Hope. He calls his niece

Mel-Mel and his nephew buddy and the idea of taking care of those kids scares him silly. I really need to speak to him. I've spent the day with Detectives Thacker and Beauchamp reviewing the videotape, but we didn't get too far. We're hoping something about the man's build might seem familiar to Quinn.''

Hope finally gave in to the persuasiveness of Oliver's voice. "Quinn's not here," she admitted.

"Why do I sense all is not well?"

"He drove out to Gloucester to get something of Kyle's."

"He's going to the house alone?"

"Yes."

Oliver swore softly. "I don't like the sound of him going in there without backup. The man on the tape was desperately looking for clues to Quinn's whereabouts. When did he leave?"

"About fifteen minutes ago."

"You hold tight, Hope. I'll try to meet him at the house." Oliver hung up before Hope could protest.

Hope stared at the phone. Had she done the right thing? Or had she put Quinn in danger by confiding in a stranger?

QUINN PARKED several blocks away and patrolled Quent's neighborhood, alert for vehicles or shadowed areas in the shrubbery that might conceal someone conducting surveillance on the house from the front or the rear. Moving silently through a neighbor's backyard, Quinn scaled the fence and dropped down into his brother's yard. Ignoring the police barrier tape stretched across the back door, he unlocked the door and entered the kitchen. The darkened stillness of the house pressed in upon him in silent reproach of the life extinguished between its walls. The house was a split-level with a family room and the laundry room downstairs in the half basement. The living and dining rooms were on the main level along with the kitchen. The bedrooms were upstairs.

Quinn switched on a small flashlight and paused when the beam swept over papers and grocery coupons littering the vinyl flooring near the desk built into the kitchen cupboard. A chill touched his spine at the sight of the upended drawers piled on the desk. The police Identification team had combed the house for evidence, but Ident teams in Quent's experience were meticulous and conscientious about neatly stacking or piling personal belongings they'd sifted through. The mess they left behind was usually limited to powder and chemical residues, not this type of disarray.

Had someone else ransacked the house after the Ident team had left? Careful not to touch or disturb anything beyond his avenue of approach, Quinn moved into the living room. The TV, compact disc player and the tower of Carrie's CDs were right where they should be. But Quent and Carrie's bedroom showed evidence of a similar rapid search. Clothes had been pulled from their dresser drawers and thrown haphazardly onto the bed. Quinn avoided looking at the bed. The Ident team had stripped it and portions of the mattress had been cut away. A glance into the master bath told him someone had rifled the medicine cabinet.

A noise sounded faintly in the house. Quinn froze, his senses on full alert. The furnace switched on and the hum of forced air reached his ears. He decided he'd call Detectives Thacker and Beauchamp once he was safely away.

As he passed through the family room to the laundry room he noted the books and photo albums on the carpet in front of the bookcase. Someone had been looking for personal information, not valuables. Quinn eased the door open into the laundry room, hoping Kyle's Blue Baboon would be hanging on the clothes rack. He found the stuffed toy in the dryer.

Mission accomplished.

Quinn tucked the baboon inside his jacket and stepped out into the hallway. He didn't realize anything was wrong until he felt the whopping jolt of electricity penetrate his neck. Quinn crashed to the tiled floor, helpless.

A second jolt into his hand knocked him out cold.

HOPE KEPT an eye on the speedometer, conscious of the fact she had children in the car. But the need to see Quinn and make sure he was okay was overpowering, urging her to go faster. Ever since she'd gotten off the phone with the man who'd identified himself as Oliver Wells, she'd worried that she'd made a terrible mistake. She'd tried calling her brother-in-law, but her sister Faith had answered the phone and Hope had hung up. Faith would want to know why she was calling from Halifax and what was wrong.

And maybe the caller really had been Oliver Wells and she was overreacting. She'd hated waking Kyle and Melanie. Fortunately, the motion of her minivan rocked them quickly back to sleep.

After driving through a maze of streets, Hope finally found Quent and Carrie's block. There was no sign of Quinn's car. She didn't bother checking house numbers. The moon highlighted an awning that had been erected on the snowy lawn of a gray-brick home with dramatic arched windows. Offerings of flowers were piled beneath the awning—notes and drawings attached to the bouquets. And someone had lit a large votive candle. Grief welled from deep within her and hot tears stung her eyes as she parked at the foot of the driveway. She cut the engine and waited a minute, afraid to leave the children alone in the car, but decided she had no other choice. Her throat and chest ached from the effort of trying to restrain her emotions. Had Quinn already come and gone? The house looked ominously dark; the yellow tape stretched across the front door foreboding.

Hope pulled her keys from the ignition and opened the driver's side door, leaving it open so she could hear the children if they stirred. She'd taken a few steps toward the house when the low, muffled sound of an engine running met her ears. It took her a moment to realize that the sound originated from inside the closed garage. What on earth?

She pounded on the garage door with her fist. "Quinn? It's me, Hope!" She tried pulling on the chrome handle. The garage door didn't budge. Was it her imagination or did she smell exhaust fumes?

Uneasiness wedged in her stomach and made her legs wobble as she ran around to the front door and rang the doorbell repeatedly. She pressed her face against the sidelight window, hoping to detect some movement inside the house.

Nothing stirred. She waited for what felt like eons, but there was no response.

Hope went into a full-scale panic. She looked around for something to break the window and saw several stones jutting up through the dwindling snow in the landscaped bed beside the covered entry. It took some digging with the heel of her boot to loosen a stone.

Holding her breath, Hope smashed the stone into the window. It took several tries to break through the double panes of glass so she could reach inside and unlock the front door. A voice inside her urged her to hurry as she found a light switch and flicked on the lights. She ran through the living room and dining room toward the back of the house, thinking that the access door between the house and garage must be somewhere near the kitchen.

There was no obvious access. She charged down a short flight of stairs to a sunken family room, finding another light switch at the base of the stairs. She spotted an open door that looked like it led to a hallway and mudroom. Seconds later, Hope located the access door to the garage. Beside it was another bank of light switches. Hope hit them all.

Carbon monoxide fumes choked her as she jerked the door open. Her heart stopped when she saw the figure slumped in the driver's seat of a gun-metal-gray sedan.

Quinn. Oh God! Was she too late?

Frantic, Hope looked for the control button for the garage door and found it mounted to the door frame. To her relief the automatic garage door opener rumbled into action. Fresh night air penetrated the garage.

Please, God, don't let him die, she prayed as she yanked open the sedan's door and leaned inside to turn off the engine. Her hands trembled as she pressed her fingers to Quinn's neck, searching for a pulse. She found one, but it felt very weak. Was he breathing?

The fear that Quinn couldn't live with the guilt of his brother and sister-in-law's deaths inched into Hope's soul. What kind of a solution was this?

She held her fingers to his mouth and nose. Relief cascaded through her when she felt the faint stirring of his breath. Knowing he was far too heavy for her to move on her own, Hope ran next door for help.

She knew her explanation to the wary-looking neighbor who opened his door to her was terribly garbled, but as soon as she mentioned Quinn's name, the man grabbed a coat from the rack in the hall and instructed his wife to call for the police and an ambulance. "Tell them we've got a possible suicide—carbon monoxide poisoning."

The man told Hope his name was Brady and that he was a doctor as they ran back toward the garage. Before they reached the driveway, Hope saw a flash of movement as a dark-clothed figure emerged from the street and darted across the lawn toward them, moonlight glinting off his silver hair.

Hope screamed, anticipating an attack.

The figure identified himself in an authoritative voice as Oliver Wells. "What's going on here? Is that you, Brady?"

Doors opened across the street. Hope tried to assimilate the information that this sinewy man, with leathered cheeks and dark, deep-set eyes, must be

Quinn's partner. Though retired, Hope thought Oliver was as physically fit as the day he'd first joined the force.

"It's okay, ma'am, I know him," Brady assured her, his eyes solemn behind the dark-framed glasses he wore. "You're just in time, Wells. We got a possible suicide in the garage. It's Quinn. This lady says he's her husband."

Oliver's brows drew together. "You're Hope? I told you to hold tight...." He pushed past her to the driver's side of the car. With Brady's help, Wells pulled Quinn out from behind the wheel and the two men carried him outside, laying him on the brick driveway. Quinn's face and lips were an alarming shade of cherry red. Teeth chattering, Hope dropped to her knees beside him intent on checking his vital signs again, but Brady told her to run back to his house and ask his wife for some blankets and his medical bag. "He's breathing and I've found a steady pulse. But we need to keep him warm. He'll have to be transported to hospital."

Hope nodded. As she rose to fetch the blankets, Brady unzipped Quinn's jacket and a stuffed animal appeared—a furry black creature with blue markings around the eyes. Blue Baboon!

Tears blurred her eyes and a sob caught in her throat. The sight of Kyle's toy dispelled the gripping fear that Quinn had tried to take his own life to put the children out of danger. Regardless of how it looked, Quinn wouldn't have bothered with Blue Baboon if that had been his intention.

Neighbors had started gathering in the driveway by the time Hope returned with the blankets and

Brady's medical bag. A heavy-set woman in a yellow tracksuit was standing sentry over the children in Hope's minivan. To Hope's indescribable joy, Quinn's eyelids fluttered open as Oliver and Brady lifted him onto a thick quilt. She helped tuck several other blankets around him. "You're going to be okay," she whispered in his ear, squeezing his shoulder.

Quinn's lips moved as he struggled to lift his head. "Children?" Hope barely heard him over the wail of approaching sirens.

Her heart crumbled. A hot tear slid onto her cheek. She cupped the back of his head with her hand, trying to be strong for him. "They're safe. They just need you to be their daddy." And she needed him to be her husband. "Kyle will be happy to have his Blue Baboon."

"Not safe," Quinn muttered back as if in a stupor. "Hit man got me. Stun gun."

"Don't let him win," Hope said vehemently, nearly beside herself with the fear that Quinn might not recover from the attack.

"Jesus, Brady, he's been zapped with a stun gun," Oliver exclaimed, leaning in closer. "Did you see him, Quinn?"

"No. Too dark."

"How do you feel?" Brady demanded. "Headache? Nauseous?"

"Both," Quinn managed.

As Brady and Wells tried to get more answers out of Quinn about his attacker, an ambulance and three police cars turned onto the street, lights flashing. Help at last! Worried the sirens would wake the children,

Hope reluctantly left Quinn in Brady's capable hands and darted through the crowd to the minivan with Blue Baboon clutched to her chest.

She asked the neighbors who had gathered by the van if they'd seen anyone suspicious lurking near the McClure's house.

"We've had people crawling all over the neighborhood since the McClures were found," the woman who'd been keeping an eye on Kyle and Melanie told her. "Mostly reporters going door to door asking for interviews. But some people just drive by wanting to look at the house and leave flowers."

"But some of them want a closer look," a burly man with a thick accent chimed in. "My wife, Helga, she chases reporters and photographers out of our backyard since Thursday. They climb over our fence and hide in the bushes trying to get pictures of the police working inside the house."

"We unhooked our doorbell and stopped answering the door. The media are blood-thirsty ghouls," said an angular man with a black ski cap pulled low over his forehead. "They don't really care about Carrie and Quent. They're just trying to make their deadlines with the trauma-of-the-week. One jerk reporter offered me one hundred bucks a day if I'd let him take over our master bedroom because it overlooks the front of the McClures' house. I told him to get lost. I heard they wouldn't leave the Brooks alone. Laurie and Rick went to stay with her mother until it all dies down."

"Who are Laurie and Rick?" Hope asked.

"Laurie was the one who noticed Melanie seemed to be alone in the house," the woman in the tracksuit explained. "She lives right behind the McClures and her kitchen window overlooks the back of the McClure house. She saw Melanie in the kitchen standing on the counter, pulling cereal boxes out of a cupboard. The boxes were falling onto the floor. Laurie tried calling because she was worried Melanie might fall and hurt herself. Melanie walked across the countertops and answered the phone. Laurie knew right away something was wrong when Melanie told her that her parents wouldn't wake up."

Poor Melanie. Hope glanced into the van to see if the children were stirring, tears squeezing onto her cheeks as the ambulance attendants descended from the emergency vehicle. Her dreams and her future hung in the balance with Quinn's life. Beyond the lit houses, darkness circled the neighborhood, thick and concealing. Hope couldn't help but wonder if the hit man was watching from afar to see if he'd succeeded.

TO HOPE'S DISMAY, Quinn refused to go to the hospital despite Brady's warnings that he might need to spend four to six hours in a hyperbaric chamber breathing pure oxygen to rid his system of the buildup of carbon monoxide.

Hope added her own pleas, but Quinn stubbornly insisted he was feeling better and had only passed out because of repeated shocks from the stun gun. He was staying right where he was to confer with the police. Oliver had spoken to the police officers who'd arrived first on the scene and Detectives Thacker and Beauchamp were called in. The area was being sealed off and searched. And Quinn was hopeful that forensics would pick up something from the house—a latent fingerprint, clothing fibers or other traces of evidence that could help them nail the hit man.

Unsatisfied, Brady had told Quinn that he might feel fine now, but he could experience severe neurological damage or end up in a coma a week from now if he didn't accept some treatment. He offered Quinn a compromise—a cylinder of oxygen and a bed for the night at his home. With pressure from Oliver, Quinn reluctantly agreed to put on the oxygen mask and confer with the police from the couch in Brady's family room.

Brady's wife, Nina, an energetic blonde with a wide smile who was four months pregnant with the couple's third child—they had two boys ages two and four—didn't seem the least put out by the prospect of unexpected overnight guests and a horde of cops trooping in and out of her house. She helped Hope settle Kyle and Melanie onto makeshift beds in the living room. When Kyle awoke in tears, his temperature still elevated, Nina asked her husband to take a look at him.

When Brady informed Hope that Kyle had an ear infection and sent another neighbor off to pick up a prescription for antibiotics, Hope's heart overflowed at the goodness and compassion offered to them by these people.

Her insides were still trembling. Her wedding day had been a series of catastrophes. If Oliver hadn't phoned her, Quinn could have died tonight—on their wedding night. What if she truly was a jinx and every relationship she entered into was doomed?

Hope dug her fingernails into her palms in an effort to steady her frayed emotions. It was nearly midnight now. The neighborhood was crawling with cops. An irrational part of her insanely wanted to believe that if they just made it to midnight without coming to any more harm, the jinx would be lifted and they'd all live happily ever after.

Unfortunately, the hushed arguing and grave expressions on the faces of the police detectives huddled around Quinn and Oliver in the family room warned her that she should expect tomorrow to hold more of the same madness.

At least Quinn was alive. They *still* had a chance of making their marriage into something more than a piece of paper, she told herself as Nina passed her a steaming cup of chamomile tea. Thankfully, Kyle hadn't put up much of a fuss when she'd given him a spoonful of the antibiotics, then rocked him back to sleep. Nina offered Hope a stool drawn up at the butterscotch-colored granite-topped island separating the kitchen from the family room, but Hope wanted to know what the police were doing to find Quent and Carrie's killer. Maybe they could talk Quinn into accepting their protection. Quinn rested on a hunter-green plaid couch, an oxygen mask strapped to his face. His coloring had returned to normal, but the stubborn glint in his eyes warned her he was still determined to do things his way.

Hope sighed inwardly, preparing herself for another uphill battle. Clearing her throat, she introduced herself to Detectives Thacker and Beauchamp.

Dressed in a tailored gray wool suit and a designer tie patterned with billiard balls, Thacker looked smart, assertive and capable of hustling the bad guys, if not Quinn. Beauchamp, on the other hand, with his drooping jowls and soulful brown eyes, reminded Hope of a faithful and world-weary St. Bernard. Even his tweed jacket appeared to be shedding.

Thacker shook her hand firmly. "Ah, Mrs. Mc-Clure. We've been holding off showing your husband the videotapes until you could join us. We wanted to ask you some questions first."

Hope darted a puzzled glance at Quinn, wondering what kind of questions they might mean.

Behind the oxygen mask, Quinn gave her a crooked grin that didn't quite reach his eyes. Were they hiding something from her? Or was this how cops acted during investigations?

"The kids okay?" Quinn asked her in a husky tone.

"Thanks to Nina and Brady, they're both asleep," she said, deciding she'd tell him about Kyle's ear infection when they could speak privately. She turned back to Detective Thacker, still feeling uneasy. Was she misreading Quinn? Maybe he was angry because she'd followed him to the house. "I'll do whatever I can to help, Detective."

"Did you see anyone or notice anything unusual when you arrived at the McClures' residence this evening—maybe someone sitting in a parked car?"

"No. I looked for Quinn's car, but I didn't see it."

"What about when you drove into the neighborhood? Did you pass any cars that were leaving?"

She shook her head. "Not that I recall."

Thacker's inky brows drew together as he ran a hand lightly over his fastidiously slicked hair. "What made you decide to follow Quinn to the house?"

Hope looked guiltily at Oliver and flushed. "Actually, Oliver Wells called my house and asked to speak to Quinn. He seemed to know Quinn very well and he was convincing—he mentioned the videotapes, but afterward, I don't know, I guess the situation was making me paranoid. I wondered why Oliver hadn't used the new cell phone number Quinn had given my brother-in-law this afternoon.'' Hope felt Quinn's steady gaze on her, but she couldn't look at him.

''Tom gave me the number *after* I'd decided to call Quinn,'' Oliver said by way of explanation.

''Well, you've got good instincts,'' Beauchamp told her, with a bolstering smile. ''Why don't you have a seat and tell us exactly what you did when you arrived at the house?''

Hope sat gingerly beside Quinn on the couch, holding the mug of tea between her palms as she described how she'd broken the window to get inside the house so she could access the garage. Quinn's hand settled protectively on her thigh as she spoke. The weight and heat of his hand made her intimately aware of the intense physical magnetism that they'd always shared. The very first time she'd met his gaze over the linen-draped dining table at a college friend's wedding, her blood had heated and shifted with purely sensual expectation. Ten years hadn't dulled her response to Quinn. She'd never regretted losing her virginity to him. It had been a mutual seduction of ecstatic volition, a joining of deepest desires—even if the relationship had only been temporary.

Though she tried to concentrate on answering the detectives' questions regarding her movements through the house to the best of her ability, every nerve and cell in her body was focused on the spot where Quinn's fingers absently stroked her inner thigh.

"How did he gain entry to the house this time?" Quinn asked the detectives.

"He forced open the window in the laundry area," Thacker explained. "He left us a clear bootprint on top of the dryer. We'll have the lab analyze it. It might tell us something."

Hope didn't know what they hoped to gain from knowing the hit man's shoe size. "He must have been watching the house," she said. "Some of the neighbors told me they've been chasing reporters and voyeurs off their properties since Quent and Carrie were discovered. Is there any chance the hit man might have been one of the trespassers?"

"Certainly," Thacker agreed, glancing at his partner for confirmation. "We'll work that angle, see if we can drum up some descriptions and match them to employee photos from the local papers and TV stations. I want Quinn's take on the videos first."

"What time was the break-in?" Quinn demanded as Beauchamp popped a video cassette into the VCR in the massive pine entertainment center.

"6:07 this morning," Oliver replied, shifting the leather chair he was seated in so that he could see the TV screen. "He was in and out in under three minutes."

Beauchamp pulled a face. "We got the call and had four cars there at 6:11 and he was already gone. He's a smooth operator." He turned the TV on. "The three of us have been over the tapes at least twenty times today. Maybe you'll see something we didn't.'' Beauchamp pressed the play button and Hope froze, her breath suspended in her lungs, as the figure of a man in dark clothing, a ski mask and latex gloves appeared on the screen in what was obviously the reception area.

"There he goes," Oliver narrated. "He grabbed everything that might possibly have something on it which could lead him to you: the Rolodex, message pads, the trash, even the imaging film cartridge on the fax machine.''

The man disappeared from view on the screen. Beauchamp stopped the cassette.

"Unfortunately," Oliver added, "a fax came in from Tom's office on Friday, requesting information for your will. Doris shredded the fax after it came in, but we didn't think to remove the imaging film.''

Hope felt panic trample through her body at the mention of her brother-in-law. "What's imaging film?'' she demanded, trying to understand.

"It's sort of like carbon paper," Quinn explained. "It prints the incoming fax messages, leaving behind an image of the document on the film.'' His gaze shifted to Oliver. "Has Tom been warned of this development?''

Hope was ready to tear out her hair. Were Tom, her sister and their family in danger, too?

Oliver leaned forward, his elbows braced on his knees. "Yes. I couldn't get through to his office for a couple of hours because there'd been a fire in his building while Tom was attending your wedding.''

Quinn swore under his breath. "I don't like these kinds of coincidences.''

"Neither did we," Wells said. "We met Tom at the scene. His office was left unlocked during the commotion and he was worried someone might have entered. Quinn's file was on top of his desk, but there was nothing in it that could indicate Hope's name or her address. He was very careful not to save the file containing the final copy of your will on the hard drive, Quinn. He had it on a diskette in his pocket."

Hope went absolutely numb with shock. Surely this wasn't happening. She looked down to see the herb tea quivering in the mug she held in her hands. She was trembling. Quinn's hand left her thigh and slid around her waist in a protective gesture that boosted her flagging courage.

She just wanted this to be over. She wanted them *all* to be safe. And she wanted Quinn's arm around her at night when she slept until they were both old and gray.

She glanced up from her mug of tea to meet Oliver's steady gaze.

His calm voice was more soothing than the tea. "I know you're concerned, Hope," he said. "We're not taking any chances with Tom's safety. He and your sister and their kids have departed on an unexpected vacation. As a precaution Gord's already working on a new vehicle and location for you. We have no reason to believe the hit man has learned your name. Even if he saw Quinn's file in Tom's office and figured out Quinn was getting married—the marriage license information is confidential. And Canada's Privacy Act limits the information he'd obtain by requesting a marriage record search on Quinn to the date the marriage took place. No personal information such as the bride's name or address would be released. Still, better safe than sorry. I want to reassure you that we've got a lot of resources at our disposal to keep you out of harm's way."

Hope desperately wanted to believe Oliver.

"The fire originated in a trash can in the men's room," Thacker said in a somber tone. "Looks like arson. Someone tried to make it look like it was an accident, but there's evidence an accelerant was used. We've got a lot of manpower interviewing everyone who works in the building and asking for lists of clients who had appointments around the time of the blaze."

"Was there a surveillance system in the building?" Quinn asked.

"Unfortunately, no." Thacker shrugged his broad shoulders. "But we might get a general description of someone who matches the height and weight of the person who broke into your office. Beauchamp, play the second tape."

As Beauchamp pressed a button on the remote control and the darkly clothed man on the TV screen moved ruthlessly through Quinn's office checking filing cabinets, drawers and shelves, Hope told herself that she could do anything—even walk away from her home and her day care if it meant keeping herself, Quinn and the children alive.

"Play it again," Quinn requested when the tape finished, frowning intently at the TV.

Beauchamp nodded and rewound the tape. Hope's heart lurched when Quinn directed Beauchamp to pause the tape just as the intruder entered his office.

The intruder's solid, well-proportioned frame was clearly silhouetted in the doorway.

"Anything about him seem familiar?" Thacker asked.

"Not necessarily familiar, but his general height and build match Ross Linville's. And he's certainly driven like Linville. I pegged Linville for the type who'd hire someone else to do his dirty work, but maybe I'm wrong. This guy is busting with confidence. He's cruising through our office like he owns the place, just like Linville sauntered into that bank and used his name and his family's reputation to ask for a loan and pass off those counterfeit stock certificates. He didn't think he'd get caught, and neither does the man who broke into our office. Maybe Linville wants to make this more personal than I originally presumed."

Hope's stomach clenched. She set her tea onto the pine coffee table, untouched. Quinn had told her on Friday evening that Ross Linville's trial was supposed to begin a week ago, but he'd skipped bail. "I thought there was a rumor he was in the Caribbean," she said hesitantly.

Thacker cleared his throat. "That rumor's still unconfirmed. His family insists they haven't heard from him since the day before he skipped bail."

"For all we know," Oliver opined, "Linville spread the rumor himself to cover his tracks."

Quinn interjected a question into the conversation, "Does he own any registered firearms?"

Beauchamp shook his head.

"Let's see the last tape," Quinn suggested.

Hope leaned forward as if to view the man's features through his ski mask as he stopped in front of Oliver's desk, his head swiveling from left to right as he scanned the room. The tape lasted under a minute.

"He looks as if he's searching for something in particular," she murmured when Beauchamp stopped the tape.

"Probably looking for computer disks and our files," Quinn said. "Our clients demand a high level of security. We only work on diskettes—nothing is saved directly on the hard drive and we keep all our case notes and evidence in a vault in the lab. We have a covert lab at another location. But the fact the intruder's obviously looking for information could mean the Asian syndicate or the Payday Ring hired him. The Asian syndicate might be concerned I've found out too much about their credit card operation via the bank employee they executed. But Hugh Simons, the mastermind behind the Payday Ring's banking machine/counterfeit corporate check scam, has a more immediate motive. His pretrial hearing is coming up in three weeks."

"We're checking out Hugh Simons's visitors and phone calls with the British Columbia prison authorities," Thacker told Quinn. "If he ordered the hit, he had to have gone through a third party. We're doing the same for Adrian Burkhold since he verbally threatened to kill you in front of witnesses."

Hope searched her memory, trying to force her tired brain cells to remember what Quinn had told her about Adrian Burkhold. She finally recalled that he was the New England coin collector who'd threatened to kill Quinn when he was sent to prison six months ago for counterfeiting rare gold coins. It seemed to her that there was another suspect who hadn't been discussed yet. "What about the doctor in the Dominican Republic with the phony diplomas?" she asked.

"Chavez?" Oliver's dark eyes narrowed as if surprised she knew of the man's existence. "I'm making some discreet inquiries through contacts in the Dominican Republic. We should have some information soon," he replied.

Not soon enough, Hope thought, overwhelmed by a bone-tiring fatigue and mounting frustration at all this conjecture. The man they'd seen on the videotape was nameless and faceless. He could be anyone. And he could sneak up on them anywhere—just as he'd taken Quinn off guard in his brother's house. Catching him seemed about as feasible as catching a shadow. Hope glanced at the oxygen mask strapped to her husband's face. Quinn had been so lucky tonight. How long could they keep running and hiding before their luck ran out?

As MERCY observed the activity in the McClures' neighborhood from a distance, frustration mounted inside him—twisting and slicing through his body like barbed wire.

Cops walked the streets, ringing doorbells and peering in shrubbery. Houses were lit up from top to bottom as if the light spilling from the windows could shield the inhabitants from becoming his next victims.

Normally, such activity would have stroked

Mercy's ego. But not tonight. The ambulance had been dispatched back to the hospital sans victim. McClure had survived.

And Mercy had failed again.

Chapter Seven

Hope was his wife. Quinn knew he shouldn't have any qualms about sharing a bed with her, especially a sofa bed in a very open living room, but he did. His body felt as battered and weak as if he'd reconnoitered a war zone on his hands and knees. Since he'd come to and discovered that Hope had saved his life, he'd been seized by a gripping sense of wonderment that bordered on awe. She was a damn amazing woman and the prospect of having her soft, beautiful body curled up in such close proximity to his struck him as being a bad idea—even in his strength-diminished state.

The kiss she'd given him before he'd left the house to find Blue Baboon hung ripe in his consciousness, taunting him with its forbidden sweetness. The oxygen mask might serve as a deterrent to kissing her in the places he remembered she liked to be kissed, but there was nothing to impede his hands from slipping under the oversize fuchsia T-shirt Hope was wearing as a nightgown and renewing their acquaintance with the enticing curves of her body. His palms ached to cradle the fullness of her breasts and his mouth yearned to coax the responsive buds of her nipples to pleasurable heights. He wanted to see her golden eyes widen and her breath catch as he slipped his fingers into her moist, warm softness and caressed her until she was rocking frantically against him, calling his name, her hands clutching at his shoulders, urging him to join her until they were both ready to explode.

"Quinn?" Hope's hesitant voice drifted to him in the darkness across the inches of bedding that separated their bodies.

Oh yes, being in the same bed with her was definitely a bad idea. Quinn tightly laced his fingers together across his chest and kept his eyes closed, feigning sleep. He'd been selfish once in his feelings for her, he couldn't be selfish again. Not when she had David Randall waiting in the wings.

Hope gave a soft sigh and he felt the mattress dip as she rolled over.

Quinn lay there in the darkness thinking. His feelings for Hope had nearly got him killed tonight. He hadn't been thinking straight. But then, Hope tended to have that effect on him. At least Oliver had had the presence of mind to remove the Glock from the back waistband of Quinn's jeans before Brady or Hope—or the attending police—noticed he was armed. Oliver had returned the gun after the detectives had departed last night. The gun now rested securely under Quinn's pillow. Only a few more days, he told himself. Just long enough for Kyle to recover from his ear infection, and ensure that Hope and the children were moved to a safe location. Then Quinn was going out in the open, come what may.

7:37 a.m. Tuesday

THE AROMA of ground coffee lured Hope from a deep sleep. That, and the sound of children singing a "Sesame Street" tune. Slowly, her eyes fluttered open. Her surroundings didn't seem familiar. Where was she? She lifted her head off the pillow, her eyes adjusting to the gray morning light seeping into the room through the white privacy sheers at the window. Quinn's half of the bed was empty. Her heart started to pound with remembered terror at the close call he'd had last night. Had he grown worse during the night?

She threw back the covers and nearly ran into the back half of the house. Kyle, Melanie and two towheaded preschool-age boys with wide grins were singing the alphabet, and having a breakfast of cereal and juice.

A lump of relief formed in her throat when she turned and saw Quinn sitting at the kitchen table with Brady, devouring a plate of muffins. The oxygen mask was gone. Though his damp hair and smooth jawline indicated he'd showered and shaved, Quinn was wearing the same loose-fitting Senators sweatshirt and jeans he'd worn the night before. And he looked just as stubborn as he had last night. There was no sign of Nina. But Hope could hear water running in an upstairs bathroom.

"Good morning," she said as Brady jumped up from his chair and offered her a cup of coffee and breakfast. She followed him to the coffeepot. "How are the patients this morning?"

"They're both recovering. Quinn and I were just

discussing symptoms he should be on the lookout
for—''

Quinn interrupted him in a clipped, obstinate tone.
''I'm fine. Kyle's doing okay, but he's still got a
slight fever. The doc here showed me how to give
him another dose of the antibiotics. He told me Kyle
should be feeling better within twenty-four hours, but
we have to give him the antibiotics until the bottle is
empty.''

Hope nodded. She'd received Quinn's underlying
message loud and clear. Quinn had warned her he
meant to leave when Kyle was feeling better and he
obviously intended to follow through with that decision. She felt like an old shoe that had been discarded because it had served its usefulness.

The feeling only intensified after she'd kissed the
children good morning, breakfasted and showered.
Hope found Nina in the living room holding Kyle
while Quinn helped Melanie on with her jacket and
boots. Quinn's and the children's emergency bags
were on the marble foyer floor. Hope added her bag
to the pile. Quinn told her that they would be leaving
soon—Oliver was getting ready to execute the
change of vehicles. ''Detectives Thacker and Beauchamp are next door. Forensics has finished combing
the house and I want to have a look inside. We've
got a few minutes if you want to gather some of the
children's belongings,'' he offered, gazing at her with
those indecipherable gray eyes. ''We can take a couple of small boxes. It won't be much, but it'll be
something.''

Hope had to bite her tongue. She felt sick inside.

How on earth could she reach him through the crushing mass of guilt he was carrying on his shoulders?

"We'll watch Kyle and Melanie," Nina offered, before Hope could protest that she thought one of them should stay with the children. "Brady and Robby are bringing up some boxes from the basement. Then they're going to take Melanie into the backyard to play. Christopher's staying inside with Kyle." As if guessing Hope's thoughts, she added, "I've baby-sat Kyle and Melanie before for Carrie." Tears clouded Nina's hazel eyes as she rubbed Kyle's back.

Hope hugged her. "Thank you. Carrie was lucky to have such wonderful friends and neighbors."

Quinn didn't say a word to her as they walked next door. Had they run out of words to say to each other? Or was their future as inevitable as the shattered window and the fragments of glass littering the front step? Detectives Thacker and Beauchamp were talking in the living room. Beauchamp was wearing the same rumpled tweed coat he'd had on the previous night. Thacker had traded the gray wool suit for a crisp navy suit with a tie sporting a golf green. Both men had dark rings under their eyes.

"Is everything all set?" Quinn asked.

"Just about." Thacker checked his watch. "We're leaving in seventeen minutes. We've got road blocks all set up. You'll have more security than the prime minister."

Quinn handed Hope the boxes and pointed her toward the stairs. "Mel's room is the first room on the right. Kyle's is the middle room. There's a family room at the back of the house with a few more toys.

I'll give you a hand as soon as I've had a look around with the detectives.''

"Okay." Seventeen minutes didn't leave much room to argue.

Hope tried not to get emotional as she opened the children's dresser drawers and closets, tried not to give in to the aching grief that constricted her heart. Kyle's room was decorated with trucks. Bunnies frolicked on the wallpaper in Melanie's room. She grabbed extra clothes and books and small toys that looked as if they were played with often. But where were the dolls Melanie had talked about?

And she wanted pictures of Quentin and Carrie. Who knew when they'd get another chance to pick up these precious mementos?

Hope hurried downstairs to the sunken family room. The photos she'd seen scattered on the rug last night were gone. Had they been seized as evidence? She grabbed a framed family photo from the shelf and stuffed it into one of the boxes. Quinn must have some photos. She was gathering all the dolls she could find when the door to the back hallway that led to the garage swung open. Her stomach lurched as Quinn and the detectives entered the family room.

She recognized the detached, invincible-as-stainless-steel expression plastered on Quinn's face. He'd worn the same look when he'd broken off their engagement ten years ago. Oh God, was their marriage over before it had even truly begun?

"Are you ready?" he asked, his voice emotionally distant and controlled.

"Yes." She tried to be just as controlled, but her heart was racing.

"We'll be leaving in the detectives' car. I'll look after loading our gear and the car seats. You get the kids."

Hope left the house without a word. Brady waved at her, immersed in a conversation about a patient on his cell phone when she entered his backyard. Melanie and Robby were playing near the garden shed. Melanie, pretending to be a rabbit, hopped into a two-foot wide space between the side of the shed and the fence.

"Come out of your burrow, little bunny. Quinn's waiting for us," Hope said, extending her hand to the little girl. Robby hopped up to her, nibbling on what appeared to be an imaginary carrot, but Hope noticed the four-year-old was pretending to eat a wooden matchstick.

"Now that's not the sort of carrot baby bunnies should be eating," she said softly. "Perhaps you should give it to me before it gives your tongue splinters."

"But Melanie gave it to me. It's magic bunny food," Robby explained.

"Well, it may look like magic bunny food, but it's actually a match and we wouldn't want you bunnies to accidentally start a fire. Where did you find it, Melanie? Were there others?"

Melanie nodded. "I found them in the bunny's burrow." Her lower lip quivered as she pulled a box of wooden matches and a gold cellophane candy wrapper from her pocket and handed them to Hope. Robby reluctantly added his match.

Hope quickly tucked the items in the front pocket of her jeans and gently warned the children that objects they picked up from the ground weren't always safe playthings. ''Robby, will you hop Melanie to the front yard, please? Quinn's waiting for her. I'm going inside to get Kyle.''

Smiling at Brady, who was unlocking the gate for Robby and Melanie, Hope climbed onto the back deck and opened the sliding glass door into the kitchen. Nina was listening to a talk show on a small TV set in the kitchen as she swept the kitchen floor. She gave Hope a welcoming smile and immediately crossed the room to turn off the TV.

Hope slipped off her boots so she wouldn't track mud into the house. ''Don't turn your show off on my account. Rosie O'Donnell's always good for a laugh.''

''I don't mind, it's going to a commercial anyway.'' As Nina spoke, staccato music flooded the kitchen signaling a station newsbreak. Nina frowned at the set as the newscaster announced the murder of an elderly minister. ''See? I certainly don't need to hear about that—''

Hope's blood turned to ice at the newscaster's mention of the Weddings of Yesteryear chapel where she and Quinn had been married the day before. ''No, don't turn it off,'' she said sharply, moving closer to hear more details. Nina was looking at her oddly. Hope felt a tremor begin deep inside her and shudder out toward her skin. What were the chances poor Mr. Drake would be the victim of a robbery the same day he'd had contact with her and Quinn? Probably about the same as a fire starting in her brother-in-law's office building.

Hope forgot all about collecting Kyle. She jammed

her feet back in her boots and ran from the house, leaving Nina calling after her. She had to tell Quinn.

FEAR. It invaded every pore of Hope's body and perched on her shoulder like a paranoid gargoyle, reminding her constantly that the hit man could, at this very moment, be on their trail. Quinn had told Kyle and Melanie as they were bundled into the detectives' unmarked car that they were going on a trip—a honeymoon. Which couldn't be further from the truth. This trip didn't have anything to do with love and new beginnings.

For the umpteenth time, Hope glanced in the passenger side mirror and checked the traffic behind them on the highway. Was that the same black pickup truck she'd seen earlier?

Her gaze riveted on Quinn's hard profile, her heart squeezing as she silently sought reassurance from the man she'd once banked all her hopes and dreams on. Anger and resolute determination were evident in the tight lines at his mouth as he kept his eyes on the two-lane highway. They were headed outside of Ottawa to a cottage in Cornwall about an hour away. The cottage was owned by another of Gord Swenson's friends. Hope wondered if she'd ever meet this mysterious Gord Swenson, who was able to provide cars and housing at the drop of a hat.

The vehicle switch to a burgundy Dodge Caravan had been accomplished on schedule without a hitch, amid promises by Oliver and Detectives Thacker and Beauchamp that Nina and Brady and their children would be immediately whisked into a safe hiding spot as a precautionary measure. It seemed horribly unjust that Brady and Nina had been caught up in the same web of fear for being good Samaritans.

In the seat behind her, a cow mooed plaintively, followed by the electronically simulated wail of a fire truck. Melanie and Kyle giggled uproariously and punched the buttons on the board books Hope had given them to play with.

"What will we do when we get to the cottage?" she ventured, even though she was sure she knew the answer. She just wanted to hear Quinn say it. Out loud.

"Lie low for a few days."

"W-will you be staying with us?" she asked flat out.

He shot her a hard, uncompromising look. "For a day or two. Until you're settled. I can't take the risk of getting anyone else involved."

The words washed over her, steeping her in disappointment. Hope knew the disappointment was her own fault. She'd let the hundred-watt attraction that still hummed between them raise her expectations to unrealistic levels.

To her surprise, Quinn's fingers snaked out and brushed her cheek for an instant. "You know I'm doing the right thing. Mr. Drake didn't deserve what happened to him."

Tears clung to Hope's lashes. The chaplain's black eyes had twinkled as he'd married them. He'd squeezed her hand and wished her every happiness.

She shifted in the passenger seat and lowered her tone because she didn't want the children to overhear. "I don't understand why anyone would hurt that dear old man."

"Because he couldn't take the chance Drake might be able to identify him if asked to give a description."

"Or maybe recognize him?" Hope frowned at the snow-shrouded fields and the bare stands of trees lining the roadway. "You said last night that the intruder who broke into your office yesterday had the same build as Ross Linville. Linville's face has been all over the news since he skipped bail a week ago. And his family has a high profile, too. What if Mr. Drake recognized him?"

"I hadn't considered that." The corner of Quinn's mouth jerked up into a halfhearted grin. "You're not only beautiful. You're smart, too."

Hope couldn't stop the frisson of pleasure that warmed her body at the unexpected compliment.

A shrill screech rose from the back seat, shattering the moment. "Mine!"

"No, mine!" Kyle insisted.

Hope turned around to see the children engaged in a tug of war over the farm animal sounds book. The truck sounds book had fallen to the floor of the minivan.

She was in the midst of retrieving the book and negotiating a truce when Quinn expelled a hoarse moan of disbelief. "Oh, Christ, hold on!"

Hope twisted around, dread rising like heated mercury to her heart. Ahead, a huge tractor-trailer had crossed the center line and was bearing straight toward them.

QUINN REACTED quickly, calculating the best means of avoiding a collision without ending up in one of the ditches bordering the highway. He swerved into the oncoming lane and pressed on the gas, aiming for the narrow shoulder on the opposite side of the road and praying the red tractor-trailer wasn't concealing any traffic behind it. His heart stopped beating as several seconds sped by. Noise roared in his ears as the tractor-trailer sped past them, missing them by centimeters. Eyes trained on the rearview mirror, Quinn saw the black pickup behind them barely avoid a collision, as well. The tractor-trailer straightened and returned to its own lane, but it was already too far away for Quinn to read the license plate.

Quinn released the breath he'd been holding. "That was too close," he muttered, casting a glance over his shoulder at the children. Kyle and Mel were looking at him with wide eyes. Kyle was clutching his Blue Baboon. "Did you see the big red truck, guys?"

"I don't like trucks," Melanie complained, pouting.

"Again?" Kyle said, somewhat hopefully, his brows lifting like question marks.

"Sorry, buddy, we won't see that truck again," Quinn replied. That was for damn sure. He gripped Hope's jean-clad knee, needing to reassure himself they were all in one piece. Her knee was trembling. Being alive had never felt so precious to him. "You okay?"

"Yes." Her voice was breathless. "I think we left my heart back there in the ditch."

Quinn was tempted to tease her, to tell her that if that was indeed the case then they had to go back and retrieve it because as of yesterday, her heart belonged to him, but he wasn't in any position to make any claims. Unease was forming a tight waxen ball in his stomach. Was it a mere coincidence that that tractor-trailer had nearly run them off the road? Quinn wasn't taking any chances with his family. He passed Hope the map Oliver had left in the vehicle. "We're changing our plans. We're getting off this road and heading somewhere else."

"Why?" she asked.

"Because that was too close."

"Surely you don't think that was…*him*," she faltered.

"I don't see how it could be—unless there's a tracking device on the car." Quinn suddenly pulled over to the side of the road. What if there *was* a tracking device hidden on the car?

"What are you doing?" Hope demanded as he checked the glove compartment for a flashlight.

"I'm going to look underneath the car for a tracking device. You study the map. Find us a place to go."

Quinn slid under the van. The ground felt like a frozen granite slab beneath him as he shone the light on the van's underbody and examined the tire wells, his ears cocked for any peculiar noises in the passing traffic.

Satisfied there was nothing hidden beneath the van, he checked the perimeter of the vehicle, running his fingers beneath the bumpers. Then he opened the rear doors where he'd stowed the boxes Hope had packed for the children. Was it possible the hit man had hidden a tracking device in one of their toys? It was a long shot, but Quinn wasn't willing to risk putting their lives on the line if he was wrong.

Hope climbed out of the vehicle and joined him. At her questioning gaze, he explained what he was doing and told her what to look for. Her face was ashen as she bent over the boxes, but she remained cool-headed.

"I have a suggestion as to where we could go. A few years ago, Tom and Faith stayed in a bed-and-breakfast on a farm in Smiths Falls. Their kids loved it. Unfortunately, I don't remember the name."

"No problem. We'll find it." Quinn carefully checked the apron pockets in a rag doll with an old-fashioned bonnet and tried to give a patient response to Melanie's imperious demands to know what they were doing back there. His niece didn't like his explanation that they were repacking the car.

"I want to go-o. *Now!*"

"We'll go soon, Mel-Mel, but first you have to sing me the alphabet. The car needs alphabet gas. What comes first, a or g?"

To his relief, the distract-with-a-question technique he'd borrowed from Hope worked, and Melanie promptly launched into song. Quinn couldn't believe he was standing by the roadside supplying missing letters to the alphabet, while he was searching for tracking devices.

Part of him hoped that Hope would join in or take over distracting the children, but she remained silent, focusing on the task at hand. Anything that was even remotely suspicious—a repaired seam in an item of clothing or the damaged spine of a book—Quinn ruthlessly set aside in a box which he planned to drop in the trash receptacle of a gas station they'd passed five minutes earlier.

But a feeling of urgency continued to hover over him after they'd discarded the box and had turned west off Highway 138 to Highway 43. When Kyle noisily started to resent being constrained in his car seat, they made a brief stop in the small town of Chesterville to buy food, change Kyle's diaper and give him another dose of medicine.

A gas station attendant in Smiths Falls directed them to Kirkland Farms, situated on a twenty-hectare tract bordering the ice-encrusted Rideau River. Marion Reeves, the chatty, ginger-haired proprietor who spoke with a slight Scottish accent, and her husband Jacob, a crusty Scot with a long face and a stiff right leg, assured them they had a vacancy and could accommodate families. Built for a wealthy mill owner and his family of eleven children, the handsome gray stone farmhouse had been constructed by stonemasons who'd worked on the Rideau Canal. While Marion babbled on about the petting zoo in the barn and the meal service that was available, Jacob squinted at the alias ID Detective Thacker had offered and readily pocketed Quinn's genuine cash. Then Marion showed them upstairs to a suite with adjoining rooms, including a crib for Kyle.

Marion handed Quinn the room key as Kyle and Melanie raced from one room to the other with Hope, whose animated reaction to every closet door and dresser drawer that was yanked open made the accommodations sound as exciting as a trip to Disney World.

"There's a play area downstairs on the sunporch

for the children, Mr. Garret,'' Marion said. ''Enjoy your stay.''

''We will.'' Quinn took the key. The fatigue he'd been holding off all day gnawed deep in his bones. He closed the door after Marion and leaned against it, feeling the security of the Glock pressing against the curve of his spine. With a giddy cry that pierced Quinn's eardrums, Kyle launched himself onto the antique double bed facing the fireplace, grunting as he scaled the frilly coverlet.

Kyle's expression was obdurate as he planted his solid little body amid the pile of lace-edged pillows stacked at the head of the bed. ''Mine.''

''I don't think so, buddy,'' Quinn said with a laugh, crossing the room. ''That bed is mine and Hope's. You and Blue Baboon have a cage in the other room.''

Quinn fell onto the bed and playfully wrestled Kyle out of the pillows, allowing his nephew to straddle his chest and pin him to the bed.

Kyle chortled his triumph. Melanie skipped in from the other room to join in the fray. Quinn groaned, half in exaggeration, half in actual pain, as Melanie's hands and feet found purchase on varying parts of his body. He glanced up from beneath the ruffle of a pillow to see Hope standing over him, her hands on her hips, a timid smile curving her lips.

As their eyes linked, color stained her cheeks, reminding him of the first glance they'd exchanged across the dining table at his friend Pete's wedding. Those golden eyes had shone with questions then, too, and he'd been young and cocky enough to think he had all the answers. Age and experience had taught him that there were some questions you couldn't put into neat little boxes. Sometimes there were no pat answers.

"Is there room for me?"

It was a potent question: part innocence, part double entendre. Quinn grinned up at her, considering his options, including the one that sprang instantly, and painfully, to mind. Maybe the best way to let off steam in an insane situation was to act a little crazy yourself. And there was no denying that something about Hope made him undeniably crazy. He reached for her hand and pulled her down onto the bed, the soft parts of her body wreaking their own torture on the harder parts of his as she joined in the roughhousing, her laughter mixing with theirs. Quinn had no trouble imagining how the original owner of the farmhouse had fathered eleven children in a bed this size. He just wanted to make it through the night— with Hope.

9:21 p.m. Tuesday

TO HOPE'S RELIEF, the children were fast asleep when she went to check on them ten minutes after putting them to bed. The antibiotics had done the trick and Kyle's fever was completely gone. One small storm weathered.

Of course, there was always another storm brewing on the horizon.

Hope paused before the partially opened door that connected the children's room with their own, her breath catching in her throat as Quinn pulled his sweatshirt over his sleek, dark head. The grimace from the effort told her he was feeling more side effects from his encounter with the hit man last night than he was letting on to.

He could use a good night's sleep, too. So could she. But sleep was far from her mind. The harshly defined ridges of Quinn's shoulders and chest rippled and gleamed in the yellow glow cast from the bedside lamps. A provocative arrow of jet-black hair feathered from a palm-size mat at his sternum past his navel and disappeared beneath the waistband of his faded jeans.

Her memory stirred, reminding her of the scent and taste of his skin. Of the feel of those crisp silken hairs. She jerked her gaze from his body to the rumpled, linen-draped bed. Her feet grew metal cleats that bit into the rug, preventing her from entering the room. She and Quinn had shared a bed last night, but this was different, and much more private. It would be just the two of them. And the thought made her decidedly nervous.

Quinn turned and draped his sweatshirt on the bed, and Hope saw the gun nestled in the small of his back. Her pulse leapt in shock, then anger, as he removed the weapon and rolled it in his shirt.

She pushed the door open with the flat of her hand and marched into the room, stopping at the foot of the bed.

Quinn stiffened. Caution banked in his eyes.

"Did I just see you hide a gun in your shirt?" she hissed, glaring up at him.

"Possibly."

"Possibly? Quinn, why didn't you tell me you

were armed? What if the children had found it? They could have hurt someone else or themselves.''

"I've been careful."

She folded her arms over her chest. "It doesn't matter how careful you are. Accidents happen. You should have told me."

"I decided it was better not to tell you because I'm carrying it illegally."

"Illegally? You mean it isn't registered?"

"Of course it is. But I'm not licensed to carry it on my person like this. I only have a permit to transport it between my house and a shooting range. I'll be up a proverbial legal creek without a paddle if I'm caught carrying it. It's hard to predict how sympathetic a crown prosecutor would be if I have the misfortune to kill this bastard in self-defense."

Her mouth dropped open. "You had it yesterday with all those police around?"

He nodded.

Hope pressed her lips together tightly. "Great, now you're risking your career and your life. Is there anything else you think I'm better off not knowing?"

He hesitated slightly, then shook his head.

Hope stared at him, wondering about that slight hesitation and wishing for once in her life she could read his thoughts. He was completely exasperating. How could she not love a man who would risk his reputation, a criminal record and his very life to protect those he loved?

But then again, she reminded herself sourly as she grabbed her pink sleepshirt and toiletry bag and stormed into the bathroom, love had nothing to do with their current arrangement. He hadn't sought her out deliberately. He'd happened upon her by chance. And that knowledge still hurt more than she cared to admit.

When she came out of the bathroom, the lights were off—except for one left burning on the bedside table. Quinn was already in bed, his back turned to her. His deep, even breathing suggested he was asleep. Hope gingerly climbed into bed, snapped out the light and rolled onto her side on the far edge of the bed. She ran her thumb along the gold wedding band Quinn had given her. Jinx or no jinx, their marriage had lasted for two whole days. It was something to be thankful for. At least they were safe for tonight.

But that didn't stop the anxiety from relentlessly churning in her stomach. Her mind fabricated all sorts of terrible things that could happen to Quinn when he returned to Ottawa until exhaustion finally dragged her into oblivion.

She wasn't sure what woke her several hours later—the electronic chirping of her cellular phone or Quinn's hand shaking her shoulder.

"Wake up, Hope. Your cell phone's ringing," Quinn mumbled huskily in her ear. "It could be Oliver."

The awareness that she was blissfully cocooned against his side, her fingers hooked over his hip, befuddled her mind. "Huh?"

Before she could sit up, Quinn leaned over her, his bare abdomen leaving a heated imprint on her flesh as he snagged her purse from the bedside table on the third ring. Hope definitely felt wobbly as he pressed the phone into her hand.

"Hello?" She blinked, trying to get her bearings

as Quinn suddenly switched on a light. The words filling her ear seemed unintelligible at first, like something out of a science-fiction movie. Someone from a security company was informing her they'd received a signal and asked for her name and her personal identification code.

Hope came to earth abruptly, finally realizing what they were talking about. She dug her fingernails into Quinn's forearm. Oh God, someone had broken into her house.

Chapter Eight

The thought of the hit man invading her home made Hope's skin crawl. What if Quinn hadn't insisted they seek out another location?

She drew her knees to her chest and wrapped her arms around her legs as Quinn issued directions to the security company to call the police, cautioning them that the intruder could be armed. Then, he punched in Detective Thacker's phone number.

Hope's imagination leapt forward. Was the hit man rifling through her drawers—just as he'd searched Quent and Carrie's home and Quinn's office—hoping to find bills, addresses and private letters that might give him leads to friends and family members who could be sheltering them? It scared her to think that hours from now, the hit man could be parking outside her parents' home or one of her sisters' homes.

Please, God. Let them catch him this time, she prayed, rocking back and forth on the bed.

Quinn switched off the phone and ran his fingers through his hair. "He'll notify us as soon as he can. We just have to wait."

Wait.

It struck her that all of her adult life she'd been waiting. Waiting to find the lasting true love that other women found. Waiting to hold her children in her arms. She was tired of waiting. And tired of continual disappointment.

Fifteen minutes later, her cell phone chirped again. Hope nearly fell off the bed. Quinn answered it this time. Her pulse dipped. She could tell by the muscle tightening in his jaw that the news wasn't favorable.

"They didn't get him, did they?" she said flatly when he finished.

"No, he slipped through their fingers. But he was definitely our man. Thacker said there was evidence he was on a scavenger hunt for information."

Disappointment tasted acrid on her tongue. She struggled to stay calm. Think. "Does that mean the tractor-trailer that nearly hit us was a coincidence? Or is more than one person after us?"

Quinn shrugged as if to say—did it matter?

The unspoken reality was that whoever was hunting him down wouldn't stop until the job was completed. They both knew the nightmare wouldn't end until he was dead. It hung between them like a guillotine poised to drop. A shudder ripped through her body and she clasped her arms tighter around her knees, squeezing them to her chest in an effort to control the fear that threatened to shatter her. She should have told him about her jinx on Friday. Let him marry someone else. He had a right to know about the risk he was taking. Matthew had died.... A tear slipped off her cheek and plopped onto her kneecap. She scrubbed at it with her fingers, banishing it. Another tear hit her other kneecap. Then another.

Her emotional axis tilted as Quinn's arms settled around her, anchoring her firmly against him. He didn't say a word, just held her. Her cheek made contact with his chest and Hope felt the strength and heat of him sear into her like the sun's warmth emanating from a stone on a hot summer's day. Life-giving warmth.

A sob rose from deep in her belly and stuck in her throat. He was her heart's most secret desire. And she couldn't lose him. Not now. Not again. She had to tell him what he was up against. Had to tell him she was jinxed.

"Oh, Quinn, I never should have agreed to marry you." The words tumbled out of her mouth on the tail end of a sob she couldn't hold back any longer. And the words kept coming, so fast between her sobs she could barely control them. She told him about her broken engagement to Steven and about Matthew's death three weeks before their wedding.

"I didn't want to fall in love with David," she babbled into his chest, afraid to look at him, afraid to see the judgment in his eyes, "but he brought me raspberry jelly donuts—you of all people should know what a sucker I am for raspberry jelly donuts." An image of sucking raspberry jelly off Quinn's fingers appeared unbidden to her mind accompanied by a bittersweet pang of nostalgia. "And David wanted a family as much, if not more, than I did. He suggested we elope and I agreed because I was worried something might occur to upset our plans—and I just couldn't face my parents and my sisters again if that happened." She couldn't face their sympathy and their concern or the kind remarks meant to make her feel better, that only made her feel worse. "I'm not even sure I was surprised when David's ex-girlfriend Susan showed up at the chapel.... I mean, I'm used to Murphy's Law ensuring that everything that can go wrong will go wrong whenever I contemplate marriage."

She drew in a ragged breath and swallowed her pride. "And then you landed on my doorstep, and the children needed me and I couldn't tell you because it sounded so ridiculous. Then everything started unraveling. We got a flat tire. Kyle got sick. I never thought we'd make it to the wedding, and when we did, I hoped it would break the jinx, but it didn't. All these other things started happening. The minister was murdered. You nearly died of carbon monoxide poisoning. That tractor-trailer almost hit us yesterday. And now, my house getting broken into. I know it sounds stupid and superstitious, but even though we actually managed to get married, I'm terrified you're going to be killed because you had the misfortune to get involved with me."

Quinn was flabbergasted. It was the most absurd, albeit endearing, confession he'd ever heard. He started to shake, not from laughter, but from the sheer irony of his life. He was going to fail her, not once, but twice, and she was going to bear the brunt of the consequences. That knowledge caused slivers of pain to wedge deeply into the unbearable guilt already filling him over the part he'd played in his brother's and sister-in-law's deaths.

"Don't you dare laugh at me, Quinn McClure."

He hooked her chin with two fingers. "Look at me," he commanded, struggling to control his feelings. He nearly groaned aloud at the glimmering golden jewels fringed by long, damp lashes she reluctantly raised to meet his gaze. Her face was pink and streaked with moisture, but Quinn thought she'd never been more beautiful. More tempting. Why was life filled with so many hard choices—every damn one of them a grueling test of honor?

"I'm not laughing at you," he said harshly. "I'm laughing at myself for being selfish enough to consider your so-called jinx to be my good fortune."

Hope sniffed. "You have a very twisted sense of logic if you think being hunted down by a hit man is a stroke of good fortune."

Quinn laughed dryly. "I was referring to the incredible odds of finding you again." His fingers traced the delicate lines of her throat to the ribbed neckline of her T-shirt. He could see her pulse fluttering wildly in the hollow above her collarbone. He wanted to dip his tongue into that sensitive niche and feel her response. He ruthlessly pushed the thought away and struggled not to give in to the desire that she had unleashed in his body the moment he'd seen her again. "Besides, I distinctly remember you telling me on more than one occasion that I was going to get myself killed one day. You hated my being in the RCMP, you just never wanted to admit it. Just like you never wanted to acknowledge my doubts about having a family."

She made a face. "Great. Now I'm psychic, superstitious *and* I have a terminal case of denial."

"No," his tone lowered and the words came from the depths of his soul. "You were, and still are, an incredibly bewitching and caring woman who knew what she wanted out of life, and I had too much respect for you to ask you to put your dreams on hold indefinitely while I pursued mine. I might not even have realized what I was doing if my father hadn't been killed just after we got engaged.'' Quinn found a peculiar sense of release in being able to talk this way, to lay old hurts to rest. ''My mom just came unglued. I never realized until that moment how resentful and unhappy she'd become while we were growing up, always waiting for my father to come home safely from one mission or another. Even when he was home, he was never deeply involved in our lives. Half the time he couldn't remember what grade we were in or the name of the hockey and baseball teams we played on.

''My mom had all these dreams for their retirement—they were going to travel and do all the things they never had time to do—and they never came to fruition. She hid her feelings from him and from us. I'm so much like my dad, I didn't want to disappoint you like he disappointed my mother. You had so many expectations…and I just knew deep down I couldn't live up to them. That's why I broke off our engagement.'' Quinn thought of David Randall. Hope's fiancé had come back to beg her forgiveness. Who knew, they might even have reconciled and gone through with their plans to elope if Quinn hadn't dropped uninvited into her life. ''I didn't want you ever to resent me or regret marrying me.''

''I could never regret being entrusted with Kyle and Melanie. I doubt your mother ever regretted having you and Quent, no matter how unhappy she was in her relationship with your father.''

She placed her left hand on his chest and Quinn felt his skin ignite at her light touch. The gold wedding band he'd given her glinted softly on her slim finger, a reminder of the one-sided promises he'd solemnly made that would most likely leave her a widow with two children.

He grinned ruefully, gently disagreeing with her. "I'm sure she regretted giving birth to us the day our snow fort collapsed on our heads and she dug us out with a shovel, not to mention the weekend we got lost in the woods on the Scout camp-out trip. Or the week we were expelled from school for lighting a firecracker in the girls' bathroom, or the time we burned down her garden shed when a science experiment went wrong." His mother had died of pneumonia shortly after Melanie's birth, and Quinn would be eternally grateful she'd never know he was responsible for his twin's death. Or Carrie's.

Hope's chin shot up. "Your mother adored you both. If she ever experienced a regret, I'm sure it was only during a moment of temporary insanity."

Temporary insanity. That aptly explained his feelings for Hope. All he had to do was touch her and logic fled, overridden by memories of the incredible lovemaking they'd once shared. Quinn clasped her left hand and kissed the ring he'd slipped on her finger the day before. No one deserved to be loved and cherished more than she. "You're the only woman I've ever wanted to marry and ten years hasn't changed that, Hope Fancy."

"McClure. The name's McClure now and don't you forget it." The smile that touched her lips and rose to glow in her eyes was his undoing.

Quinn couldn't stop himself from threading his fingers through the silken strands of her hair, from crushing his mouth to hers. Need exploded in the core of his being and spiraled through him with centrifugal force. She tasted of remembered joy and desperation and the forbidden sweetness of temptation.

He kissed her hungrily, wanting to forget everything but the breath-stealing exhilaration of being with the woman he'd never been able to completely forget, much less eradicate from his heart.

Her tongue teased and tormented him, leading him down a path to a quagmire he happily drowned in. He was beyond the point of no return and he didn't give a damn. His senses were filled with the scent of her hair and the exquisite feel of her.

Even though they were no strangers to each other, his heart pounded with the uncertainty of a nervous bridegroom as he slid his hands over her shoulders.

The cotton T-shirt she wore was a frustration to his purpose as he fitted a palm to one soft pliant breast. He broke their kiss long enough to pull it over her head and toss it to the floor.

Hope tilted her head back, her dark hair splayed over her shoulders, and let him look at her. Quinn thought of strawberries and cream as he gazed at the feminine perfection of her skin and the dusky nipples swelling under his gaze. The only thing she wore was a pair of white silk panties trimmed with a tiny satin ribbon at the front. He felt a sharp pang in his midsection as he made a private inventory of the delicate dips and curves of her body that required his devoted attention, and the order in which he would tend to them. But first he'd peel those panties off with his teeth.

They didn't have forever. They only had tonight and he wanted a memory to take with him to his grave. For one night she'd be his wife in every sense of the word. He touched his thumb to her lips swollen from his kisses and ran it down over her jaw to her throat on a slow descent to the satin bow trimming her panties. "You're every bit as beautiful as I remember," he said huskily, "but you still have too many clothes on."

Hope's gaze met his, sultry anticipation banking in her eyes. Her soft laugh was the sexiest thing he'd ever heard. "Some things never change. You first." He obediently rose from the mattress and stood at the side of the bed as her fingers boldly reached for the band of his black boxer shorts and eased them off over his hips. His erection swelled free of its restraint.

Quinn grinned at her wickedly before her fingers could grasp him and pushed her playfully back into the downy embrace of the pillows. "Your turn."

He knelt on the floor and parted her legs. The small gasp that escaped her lips as he nibbled the sensitive skin on the inside of her right knee encouraged his efforts. Ten years drifted away as if they were only seconds as he paused here and there to savor the delicate softness he'd always considered manna from heaven. He could feel Hope tensing as he neared the border of her panties, felt her fingers rapidly skim his shoulders and rake his hair.

Her breath quickened as he lifted her legs and hooked them on his shoulders. He tasted silk and satin as he ran his tongue along the rim of her panties.

The ribbon tickled the tip of his tongue. He gripped the ribbon with his teeth and pulled.

Hope arched toward him, the panties whisking down her thighs. "Oh, Quinn!"

Her cry turned to a soft moan as he ruthlessly tugged her panties off and let them fall to the floor beside her T-shirt. Her thighs trembled as he brushed his fingers close to the nest of dark curls and touched her with the intimacy of a lover. Slowly. Skillfully.

She was so slick and wet for him he nearly gave in to the temptation to thrust himself into her right then. Hope writhed on the bed, lifting her hips as his fingers glided in and out of her. "Make love to me," she pleaded.

"I intend to, but all in good time," he murmured, his own breathing labored as he dipped his head and tasted the moist essence of her. A smile built inside him as Hope clutched at his shoulders when he found the bud hidden in the delicate folds and probed it with his tongue.

Why was making love to her so different from making love to any of the other women he'd slept with in the past ten years? The thought was forgotten as he felt the tremors form and begin to rack her body. Feeling his own tension mounting to unbearable limits, Quinn eased his mouth from her and laved a path to her navel, detouring to taste the hollows formed beneath her pelvic bones. His hands explored the delicate bones of her ribs and finally claimed her breasts.

His thumbs brushed their swollen tips, then kneaded them to even sharper points. Hope whimpered and moved restlessly beneath him, exploring his body with her hands. When her nimble fingers finally settled firmly over his erection, Quinn knew he'd lost control of the situation.

"You're driving me crazy," he groaned, suckling her right breast.

"I think that's the whole idea," she fired back, stroking the tip of him with a finger meant to send him over the edge.

"I don't have any protection," he said, trying to grasp at anything to prevent him from giving in to his desire.

"I have a box of condoms in my bag."

He lifted his mouth from her breast and stared at her. "You came prepared?"

Her eyes glistened. "They were for my honeymoon."

Her honeymoon. It brought him back to reality.

She stroked him again with seductive determination. "Don't you dare think about stopping now, Quinn McClure. Every bride deserves a wedding night. Don't disappoint me."

Quinn couldn't think when she touched him like that. All he could do was feel. React. Sensations swirled around him. He grinned down at her. "I'll try not to—" Then he lowered his tongue to the valley between her breasts. Hope's glimmering eyes were the eye of the hurricane he was swept up in. Finally, when he could feel the storm battering hard upon him, he sheathed himself and entered her, thrusting himself in so deeply he feared he might have hurt her. But she locked her arms around his neck and her legs around his waist, sheltering him, and urged him closer still.

Quinn didn't need to be asked twice. Holding her face between his hands, he kissed her and started to move...once, twice, his thrusts escalating until they were both riding the edge of desire with wild abandon. When release came, it hit them like a wall of wind, buffeting them suddenly into a dark, motionless realm.

Hope let her body drift on the sea of tranquillity, enjoying the weight of Quinn's sweat-slicked body on hers and the thundering pounding of his heart against her ribs. She didn't want to move, didn't want to breathe, for fear of breaking the spell cast by their lovemaking. He was still inside her and she wanted the world to freeze. With a small sigh of contentment, she pressed a kiss to his neck, reveling in the salty taste of his skin. She loved him so much. Only the irrational fear that she might seal his fate with the jinx by pronouncing those feelings had kept her from crying out those three little words in the throes of their lovemaking.

"What on earth did you just do to me, Quinn Mc-Clure?" she whispered, still panting.

She instantly regretted her question when he propped himself on his elbows, taking some of his weight off her chest. He cocked an eyebrow, his sensuous lips easing into a grin that made her blood heat. "I was trying not to disappoint you. It wasn't obvious?" His hips pressed firmly into hers. "Maybe I should try again."

She laughed, feeling more contentment than she'd felt in a decade. How she'd missed him! Missed the sound of his voice and the sight of his handsome face. Missed the teasing banter they'd shared that made her feel as if they were two vines twined together, each supporting the other. And more than anything else, she missed the way he stripped her clothes off with those hungry looks that never failed to make her feel like a desirable and sexy woman. "Don't make promises you can't keep."

His eyes hardened to flint. "This is about the only promise I *can* keep to you."

A chill swept her damp skin at his brutal honesty. She knew, oh, she *knew* he was going to break her heart again. And soon. But she wouldn't trade this moment for anything. Already she could feel him swelling inside her. Could feel her inner muscles clench around him. "I don't want promises," she said, arching her hips in invitation. "I just want you. Now."

Hope met his kiss with bittersweet pleasure. He was completely spoiling her for other men.

6:54 a.m. Wednesday

HOPE EXPECTED Quinn to leave; she just didn't expect him to make the announcement within moments of her waking up in his arms the next morning.

The stubble on his jaw rasped her forehead as he brushed a kiss on her brow. "It's time to end this. I want you to drive me to a bus station after breakfast. That will give me a chance to say goodbye to the children."

"No!" Her arms tightened instinctively around his

waist. Had last night been his way of telling her goodbye? "He'll kill you if you go out in the open."

"Not if I can help it. Oliver's hiring a security team to protect me."

"How very comforting," she snapped. "Besides, you're in no condition physically to go now. We don't know if you've fully recovered from the carbon monoxide poisoning. Brady warned us you could still develop some serious side effects."

"I'm fine."

She twisted her head to look at him, already feeling the fragile bubble of intimacy between them stretching precariously thin. "No, you're not fine. You're under tremendous emotional pressure and making snap decisions without thinking about the long-term consequences. Stay in hiding with us until the police arrest the hit man. The children need you, Quinn. They need you alive." *Just like I need you,* she added silently.

He glared back at her. "I need to do this."

"Why? Is it justice you want? Or revenge?"

His jaw locked. "You know better than to ask me that."

"Do I? You're carrying a gun. You're breaking one of the laws you swore to uphold when you were a police officer. Or maybe," she said very softly, "you just want to get yourself killed—punish yourself for what happened to Quent and Carrie. I think you're less afraid of squaring off against a hit man than you are of living with the guilt of what happened and living up to your responsibilities to Melanie and

Kyle.'' She felt his body go rigid, but she didn't care. ''Which is it, Quinn?''

He met her question with dead silence. His eyes held the same stone-cold determination they'd held when he'd broken their engagement ten years ago.

As she did then, Hope knew she was fighting a losing battle. One of the things that had attracted her to him in the first place was his strong sense of ethics. Like her father, Quinn was ruled by what he felt was just, and damn the consequences.

In the other room, Kyle stirred and cried out for his mother. ''I'll go to him,'' she said sharply, climbing out of the bed. She snatched her T-shirt from the floor and pulled it over her naked body. She was so angry her limbs felt like brittle matchsticks as she crossed the room. She paused at the door to deliver a parting blow. ''Children are gifts from heaven, Quinn. They bring out the best and the worst in you. As far as I'm concerned, your loss is my gain.''

She was shaking when she entered the children's room. Kyle was trying to hoist himself out of the crib, fat pear-shaped tears dribbling down his plump cheeks. His Blue Baboon had fallen to the carpet. Melanie was still slumbering, hidden on the daybed beneath a mound of her blankets and dolls. Hope scooped up Blue Baboon, scolding him for escaping the zookeeper's cage, then greeted her nephew with a warm smile.

The feel of Kyle's squirming body as she lifted him into her arms immediately calmed her, reminding her what was truly important. She kissed his tousled curls and chased away his tears with an impromptu game of where's your nose? while she changed his diaper. For all the hurt Quinn had inflicted upon her heart, past and present, he'd given her something more precious than gold. She just had to trust him to take every precaution to save himself.

Chapter Nine

Kissing the children goodbye was more difficult than Quinn had imagined it would be. Fortunately, they were both buckled in their car seats and couldn't follow him inside the bus station. But slamming the van's door on their panicked cries gave him more than a moment's uncertainty. Hope stood stoically beside the van, waiting, her arms wrapped around her middle, her teeth clamping down on her lower lip. Something in her stance reminded him of his mother, of other strained goodbyes.

"It's not too late to change your mind," she said sharply.

Quinn swallowed hard and studied her face, memorizing the details. Her features were pale and pinched beneath the brim of her dark green winter hat—a far cry from the woman who'd laughed and sighed in his arms last night. "I'll stay in touch," he responded, resisting the urge to pull on the tails of the knitted green and rose wool scarf draped around her neck and kiss her. "You have the phone numbers I gave you?"

"Yes. Be safe."

He nodded. "Take care of the children."

There was nothing left to say. They were at a crossroads with one another. Quinn shouldered his duffel bag and walked into the station.

FOR THE FIRST several hours of his return to Ottawa, Quinn cherished his freedom and the ability to move unencumbered and to think without a shriek reverberating in his ears or a toddler beaning him with a projectile. He needed every ounce of concentration to be on the alert for anything remotely suspicious. Paranoia accompanied his movements as he asked the taxi driver to let him off a block away from his condo.

His security system informed him that there had been no intruders into his personal domain. The well-ordered, loftlike space appointed with black leather furniture and art from his travels offered the soothing serenity of a star-filled sky, but he couldn't help wondering how Hope was faring with the children.

Quinn's first order of business was to contact Oliver.

His partner answered on the first ring. "That was a fast return trip. I've been expecting your call, but not this soon. Did you get Hope and the children settled?"

"Yes." Quinn refrained from informing Oliver of the last-minute change in their destination over the phone. He'd tell him in person later. "Did you manage to finish up the report on the Butler case for me?"

"It wasn't easy, given the time constraints, but I pounded out eighty-four pages. The courier guaranteed it would arrive in Pembroke by four this afternoon.''

Quinn checked his watch. It was 1:17 p.m. ''Excellent. We can't afford to let an opportunity like that slip through our fingers.'' Hanging up the phone, he reached into a sleek ash cabinet for a telephone book and looked up the address for the Pembroke Hotel in Ottawa. It was located a few blocks from the Ottawa Congress Centre. He'd be there in Room 84 at 4:00 p.m. In the meantime, he had a few phone calls to make and favors to call in. Despite Hope's last accusation, he wasn't going down without a fight.

QUINN COULDN'T have placed his life in better hands. The private security company Oliver had hired was made up of ex-cops and former soldiers—a team of seasoned experts who provided bodyguard services for VIPs and celebrities who lived, worked or vacationed on Canadian soil.

Over the course of several hours, they hammered out a strategy and several contingency plans for keeping Quinn under constant, albeit invisible, protection twenty-four hours a day, the idea being to trap the hit man, not warn him off. Quinn was given instructions to vary his arrival time and approach to the office every day, and was equipped with a digital cell phone, a wireless panic button cleverly hidden in a pager and a bullet-proof Kevlar vest.

When the meeting was concluded and room service had cleared away the remains of their evening meal, Quinn set up the laptop computer Oliver had brought on the wooden table where they'd eaten. The diskettes containing the files he'd requested from the vault were in a clear plastic container, each diskette neatly labeled.

Oliver handed him a thick manila file. "This contains newspaper articles, magazine articles and information our ever-efficient secretary downloaded from the Internet on Ross Linville and his family. I thought you might want to start there since the man we caught on videotape breaking into our office matched Linville's height and build."

Quinn gratefully accepted the file. "You're going above and beyond the call of duty, partner. I'm afraid to ask what the going rate is these days for an elite team of bodyguards."

The stress of the last few days flickered in Oliver's lined face before he turned away, his gray head bowed as he examined the contents of the hotel room's minibar. "So we have to raise our fees or squeeze a few more cases into our schedule. We can manage. There have already been enough casualties." He offered Quinn the choice of a cola or a club soda. Neither wanted to dull their wits with alcohol. Quinn took the cola. Oliver kept the club soda and joined him at the table, rolling his shoulders as he sat down. "Do you think Hope will be okay in the cottage? I arranged to have it stocked with food and diapers."

Quinn popped the tab of his cola. "We never made it to Cornwall. A tractor-trailer nearly ran us off the road, so we changed destinations."

"A truck? How could he have managed that?" Oliver's thick silver brows drew together. "The switch was perfectly executed. He couldn't have gotten close enough to plant a tracking device."

"That was my first thought," Quinn admitted. "I checked the car and the kids' belongings that we collected in the house on the off chance he may have planted a tracking device. The car was clean and I threw out anything I wasn't one hundred percent certain was bug-free. I've got Hope and the kids holed up in a bed and breakfast in Smiths Falls. The owners are prepared to let them stay for a week or two. I took a bus into town so she would have the car."

"Well done. Hope's got a good head on her shoulders. She'll be good for you. She reminds me of my wife—pretty and sensible. And not afraid to give you guff when you need it."

Quinn had never met Oliver's wife Rachel. She'd died fifteen years ago of a stroke, but he couldn't imagine anyone giving his hard-nosed, taciturn partner guff. Oliver hadn't achieved his success and his reputation without having made a lot of tough decisions, and he'd never regretted one of them. Oliver's daughter Tracy, whom Quinn had seen a handful of times during school breaks, was in her fourth year at Queen's University in Kingston. Quinn quickly changed the subject. He didn't want to talk about Hope. Didn't want to remember her censorious expression when she'd dropped him off at the bus station or dwell on her last accusation. "Have you heard from Thacker and Beauchamp? Did forensics find anything conclusive when they went through Quent's house—or Hope's?"

"Not yet. The lab's working on it. Give 'em time."

"I made a few calls before I came here. I touched base with a contact in the Dominican Republic. Dr.

Chavez went on a short overnight trip about two weeks ago. No one seems to know where he went. I've got a private investigator in British Columbia backgrounding Hugh Simons and other members of the Payday Ring. And the president of the New England Numismatic Society, the coin collecting society, is pooling his membership and will fax me everything they know about Adrian Burkhold.''

''Thacker told me Burkhold has only had one visitor in the last six months. His sister Alice went to see him on his birthday in early December. He hasn't sent any letters or received them. The only calls he's made have been to his sister.''

''What do you know about the sister?''

''She's an ICU nurse in Philadelphia, married, five kids. Her husband teaches high-school geography and coaches the varsity basketball team. I've had an information broker check their bank accounts. No unusually large sums of money deposited or withdrawn that might be funneled toward a hit man.''

''He could have made the arrangements through a third party he met in prison.''

Oliver nodded with characteristic pragmatism and reached for the plastic box containing the diskettes. ''The possibilities are endless, my friend. Just watch your back.''

7:02 a.m. Thursday

QUINN WOULD BE LYING if he said he wasn't constantly looking over his shoulder as he journeyed to his office early Thursday morning. Though Oliver had stayed the night in the same hotel, they'd arrived by separate routes. He and Oliver had worked too late last night for him to call Hope afterward and check on the children. Or at least that's the excuse he'd given himself last night.

He'd thought about phoning her this morning when he woke up, but had come up with a handful of excuses why he couldn't call right then. She might still be asleep. She might be in the shower. She might have her hands full with Kyle and Mel. She might refuse to talk to him. Or worse, she might talk to him with more of that razor-sharp bluntness that turned him inside out and made him question himself. Every self-protective instinct he'd had drilled into him as a cop warned him that letting himself be distracted by his feelings for Hope would put him in a coffin.

Which would only serve to convince Hope that she *was* jinxed. He needed to keep his head clear and sharp. Sleeping with her had muddied the waters of their relationship, not to mention short-circuited his senses.

Quinn stared down at the list of names and references he'd culled from the articles about Ross Linville last night, aware of the silence of his office pressing in on his eardrums in a steady muffled stream as if he were standing under a waterfall. No whining, no laughter. No pint-size sticky bodies demanding explanations and hugs and offering damp kisses. None of Hope's cajoling smiles. None of her pointed questions. Only silence. And work.

Was that what his life was truly about?

Usually, at a moment of uncertainty, Quinn would call his twin. If he was in town, he and Quent would meet for a beer and catch up on each other's lives, or he'd drop by his brother's house for dinner and they'd both wrestle with the kids, as they'd wrestled with their dad when they were younger. By the time Quinn hung up the phone or returned to his condo, he was always back on an even keel. Now he wondered if he'd ever be back on an even keel again.

Quinn pushed back the wall of pain that pressed in on the emptiness inside him. The connection he'd had with Quent was irretrievably severed. They used to be able to read each other's thoughts, finish each other's sentences—though Quent, because he'd been born last, always wanted to have the last word. Sometimes they'd even sensed each other's pain when they were younger. It shattered Quinn to think the aching emptiness he felt was Quent's anguish at having his life ripped from him.

He forced his attention back to Ross Linville and the list. Linville had family, friends and business contacts all over the world. He'd likely go somewhere familiar, but not so familiar he'd be instantly recognized. But where?

The chirping of his cell phone broke his concentration. Quinn glanced at his wristwatch. It was 8:30 a.m.

"McClure, this is Detective Thacker. We just got a report back from the lab on the evidence the Ident team found in your brother's house Monday night after you were assaulted."

Quinn jabbed his fingers through his hair. "Any fingerprints?"

"Sorry, the best I can offer is information on the shoeprint we found on top of the dryer in the laundry room. They got a clear print. The lab tells me the suspect wears a size 10 boot. But the good news is that they found some carpet fibers in the bootprint which match the carpet at the Weddings of Yesteryear chapel and a small piece of red heart-shaped confetti. We found the same kind of confetti in the chapel's parking lot.''

The basket of flowers and confetti Melanie had dropped! And he'd thought his niece and nephew were hindering his investigation.

The detective laughed when Quinn told him. ''Thanks to your niece's fall and the carpet fibers, I think we can reasonably conclude that whoever killed Edward Drake was the same person who tried to kill you.''

Quinn closed his eyes. At least there was *some* evidence, even though it didn't link the killer to Quentin and Carrie's deaths.

''The lab is still working on the forensic evidence that was gathered at your wife's house,'' Thacker continued briskly. ''I should have more news by the end of the day. This case is at the top of the priority list. Unfortunately, the intruder didn't leave a footprint for us on any of the glass he cut out of the bedroom window. And he obviously knew better than to break the glass and pull the shards out with his fingers, so no fingerprints there either.''

''Which bedroom window?'' Quinn asked, wanting more details than the scant information the detective had given him over the phone the other night.

''The one over the porch. He must have used one of the porch columns for a ladder.''

Hope's room was directly over the porch. Nausea

swelled in Quinn's stomach at the thought of the hit man invading her room.

"Anyway, we think he was aware of the fact there wasn't anyone in the house. He was looking for her financial records and her phone bills. We couldn't find an address book, so we presume he took that, as well."

The information only served to confirm Quinn's gut-level belief that he'd made the right decision to surface. Quinn glanced down at the information he'd been compiling on Ross Linville which covered his desk. "My wife said something to me the other day about the chaplain's murder that I haven't been able to get out of my mind." *His wife.* How proprietary that sounded. How permanent.

"What's that?"

"I explained to her that the hit man likely killed Mr. Drake because he didn't want the chaplain to be able to identify him. She thought I meant Mr. Drake had recognized his killer and when I tried to correct her, she pointed out that Ross Linville's picture has been all over the news. Maybe Drake *had* recognized him. It's a thought worth considering."

"It's duly noted," Thacker said. "The only problem is that we haven't been able to dig up any background on Linville that would indicate he has the capability or the training to perpetrate these crimes. The man we're looking for has killed three people."

"Linville was intelligent enough to learn how to counterfeit stock certificates over the Internet. What's to stop him from acquiring similar knowledge about security systems and weapons?"

"Point taken."

They talked for a few minutes longer. Quinn told Thacker he was reviewing his files and would contact him if he came across any information he thought would be useful. And he broached the subject of luring the hit man to his brother and sister-in-law's memorial service. They discussed possible locations, security tactics and issuing a press release to the media. Quinn knew he was only receiving this level of cooperation from Thacker because the detective saw this case as a way to make a name for himself. Thacker was ambitious, and bringing a hit man into custody—especially if it turned out the hit man was an international killer and wanted in other countries—would earn the detective a lot of glory. Quinn promised to contact the funeral home and get back to him. As he hung up the phone, a blanket of grief settled over him. God, he hoped it would all be over soon.

8:41 a.m. Thursday

THE ANTICIPATION of killing always gave Mercy an appetite. This moment was no different. He smiled as the waitress placed a plate piled with fried eggs, bacon, hash browns and toast in front of him, then refilled his coffee with a flirtatious smile. The woman had breasts a man could bury his face in, but Mercy wasn't in the mood to pursue her. Not until McClure was dead. All the arrangements had been made. After breakfast he would set the wheels in motion. McClure was back in Ottawa, right where Mercy wanted him.

His cell phone beeped as he poised his fork over his plate. Annoyed, Mercy set his fork down.

"Yes?"

It was his associate Bernardo, a good man who had been useful to Mercy on numerous occasions. Now Bernardo's role was pivotal in Mercy's plans.

Bernardo's report was brief. "She's still here, boss."

"Are you sure?"

"I can see her inside the house. That's one hot-looking babe."

"Then it won't be a chore to keep her in your sight at all times. Make sure she doesn't disappear." Mercy's eyes scoured the restaurant, making sure no one was within listening range. "You move in on my orders only. Understood?"

"Understood."

Mercy went back to his breakfast with a self-satisfied smile. Much of his success could be attributed to investing in that extra bit of insurance.

THE CALL that came in at 10:12 a.m. was like so many others Quinn had received in the past: the caller identified himself as Yves Lapointe, president of a payroll services company in Winnipeg, Manitoba. Lapointe mentioned he'd become aware of the special services Quinn's company had to offer via the publicity surrounding the Ross Linville case and requested a private meeting on a confidential matter.

Lapointe spoke with gravelly, self-assured authority. "I'm in Ottawa on other business and had a last-minute cancellation. My hotel isn't far from your office. Is it possible we could meet at 11:00 a.m.?"

Quinn hesitated. That didn't leave him much time to check out the call. Was that the caller's intention? The call-display device on his phone told him the number was blocked. "You're in luck. My schedule is open this morning. Did you wish to meet here or at another location?"

"I'm staying at the Ambassador Hotel. There's a coffee shop across the street from it. Could we meet there?"

"Certainly."

"What will you be wearing so that I'll recognize you?"

The hair prickled on the back of Quinn's neck. "I've got dark hair and will be wearing a black jacket."

"I'll look forward to our meeting." Lapointe hung up before Quinn could ask any more questions.

Quinn bounded out of his chair and barged into his partner's office. "I just got a call that could be it." He quickly related the details. "The coffee shop is a few blocks away. He'll expect me to be walking over. You notify the security team and get them in place. I'm going to check out the caller."

Oliver nodded. His gaze drifted meaningfully toward the photo of his daughter on his desk. "I haven't been the best of fathers at times, but I've done my best and she's brought me joy. Are you sure you want to go through with this now that you have a wife and children to think about? You'll be a sitting duck."

Quinn had never expected Oliver to turn on him. *"Et tu, Brute?"*

"What good's a seasoned veteran if he can't impart a bit of his hard-earned wisdom on the younger generation? I'm counting on you to live to be my age.''

''Alert the team, Oliver. Time's running out.''

QUINN'S FIRST CALL was to the Ambassador Hotel. When he asked the desk clerk if an Yves Lapointe had checked in, he was told Lapointe had arrived the day before. The clerk offered to connect him to Lapointe's room, but Quinn hung up before the call could be put through.

Next he dialed directory information and asked if there was a listing for the payroll services company in Winnipeg. Quinn wanted more confirmation than that. He punched in the number.

''I'd like to speak to Yves Lapointe, please,'' he told the switchboard operator.

His heart beat painfully as he was connected to Lapointe's office.

A woman answered the phone. Quinn asked to speak to Lapointe.

''I'm sorry, Mr. Lapointe isn't available at the moment to take your call. May I take a message?''

Quinn didn't have any trouble sounding apologetic as he introduced himself. ''I just received a call from Mr. Lapointe. He asked me to meet him at his hotel this morning and I didn't realize until the call was completed that he'd neglected to give me the name of his hotel.''

The secretary laughed. ''Not to worry. He's staying at the Pan Pacific Hotel. Would you like the phone number?''

''Yes, please.''

Quinn's pulse quickened as he jotted down the number. The Pan Pacific Hotel was in Vancouver on the other side of the country. He promptly dialed the Pan Pacific and was told that Mr. Lapointe wasn't in, but they would be happy to take a message. Quinn was stumped. Was this a setup or had Yves Lapointe gone to great lengths to make sure even his secretary didn't know where he was going?

Quinn shared the information with Oliver when he came in to report that the team was in place.

Oliver frowned. "Lapointe wouldn't be the first person to keep his secretary in the dark—and wisely. More than one secretary has mastered her employer's signature for her own personal gain. We'll assume the worst and hope for the best." He laid an enlarged map of the city on Quinn's desk and verbally detailed the route the team had suggested Quinn take on foot to the Ambassador Hotel. "There are plenty of buildings he could be ensconced in with an assault rifle, or places he can step out from to get you at point-blank range. Or he could have a drive-by shooting in mind. You won't be alone."

Quinn visualized the hazardous areas as he shrugged into his jacket. The fit was more snug because of the Kevlar bulletproof vest he wore, so he left it unzipped and slipped the Glock into his jacket pocket.

It was fourteen minutes to eleven.

He deeply regretted not calling Hope.

Pushing an image of her to the bottom-most corner of his heart, Quinn shook his partner's hand, then walked down the hall to the elevator. The doors slid open almost instantly with a faint ding. The elevator was empty. Less than a minute later, Quinn crossed the tiled foyer of his office building and stepped outside into the brutal chill of a gray March morning.

Chapter Ten

Quinn had the curious sense he was viewing the dismal slush-filled Ottawa street through a wide-angle camera lens, focusing on the whole picture from the top of the modest skyscrapers to the pedestrians picking their way along the icy sidewalks. Snow that had been charming and white during the winter had been transformed, churned into somber shades of gray and brown. His ears filtered the noise of the street traffic, detecting the slapping of boots on concrete, the swish of a revolving door, the screech of air brakes from a bus and snippets of conversation.

He recognized members of the security team emerging from doorways, riding by on a courier's bike, offering him a sausage from a vendor's cart. Quinn stopped at the corner and waited for the light to change, eyeing the drivers in the eastbound lane with caution. No engines gunned as he stepped into the crosswalk.

About halfway down the block on the opposite side of the street, a black sedan pulled into a no parking zone in front of a fire hydrant. Quinn's nerves were on full alert. He saw a member of the security team casually cross the street toward the car. He was momentarily distracted by the tinkling of a shop bell and swiveled his head to see an elderly woman in a camel wool coat leaving a bookstore. A knitted wool cap covered her head and a pair of dark-tinted lenses concealed her eyes. Her thick legs were encased in opaque tights. She gave him a timid smile as she negotiated a slippery patch of sidewalk in front of the store.

Quinn could feel his heart beating as if it were an echo, the source originating a kilometer away. He gave the woman a brisk nod, his gaze trained on her hands. She turned in the opposite direction. He paused in front of the window of a gentlemen's clothiers for a few seconds, watching her progress.

She moved slowly and steadily. When he was satisfied she posed no threat, he continued down the street. The car that had pulled over was easing back into traffic. Quinn felt his muscles tensing as the car passed. The driver didn't even look at him.

Only two more blocks.

A man in a charcoal-gray trench coat, hands jammed into his pockets, nearly bumped into him at the next intersection. He was wearing headphones that were obviously plugged into something in his pocket. Quinn glared at him. "Watch it."

The man backed away, his pale eyes widening. "What's your problem?"

"No problem. Just watch where you're going."

The hotel was around the corner on his right, the coffee shop just across the street. Quinn kept a sharp eye on the intersection as he approached, noting the positions of other members of the team.

There was no sudden squeal of tires as he crossed the street. Could this all be a false alarm?

He yanked open the door of the coffee shop. The interior smelled of bacon grease, fresh-roasted coffee and damp wool. No one was waiting on the orange vinyl bench near the cashier. Quinn scanned the customers at the tables. No one glanced at him as if trying to identify him.

He checked his watch. It was dead-on eleven.

He decided to wait. If this was a legitimate appointment, Lapointe could be running a few minutes late.

Quinn waited fifteen minutes, grinding his teeth while he waited. At five minutes past the hour, one of the team members entered the café and ordered a coffee at the counter.

Quinn pulled out his cell phone and called Oliver. "He's a no-show. I'm going across to the hotel. I'll ask for him there."

When he helped himself to the courtesy phone in the lobby he was informed Lapointe had checked out.

A sick feeling rolled through Quinn's gut. He scanned the lobby, searching for anyone who might covertly be watching his movements. Was this all a misunderstanding or had someone just sent him on a wild-goose chase?

Quinn found an isolated corner of the lobby and called Detective Thacker on his cell phone. He wanted answers fast, and Thacker had the authority to get them.

12:53 p.m. Thursday

MORE THAN twenty-four hours had passed since Hope had dropped Quinn at the bus station. He hadn't called—not even to ask after the children. Was he sending her a message? The other night, before they'd made love, he'd told her he'd broken their engagement because she'd had too many expectations of him. It sobered her to acknowledge that maybe he was right.

With a sigh, Hope checked the diaper bag to make sure she had everything she needed for an outing into town this afternoon with the children. There was a Hershey's chocolate factory that offered tours, and she'd figured that keeping Kyle and Melanie busy and entertained would keep them from wondering when Quinn would return. She hoped the same prescription would work for her. The antique bed which had seemed so narrow when she and Quinn had shared it had felt enormously wide last night.

Melanie and Kyle were currently bouncing on the same bed, pretending it was the big comfy couch in the show they were watching on television. Hope glanced at her watch. The show would be over in a few minutes, then they'd leave. She scanned the room for forgotten articles, wondering where she'd put the key to their room when they'd come in from petting the sheep and the goats in the barn. She felt a lump in the right front pocket of her jeans. Slipping her hand into her pocket, she pulled out the wooden matchbox and the gold cellophane candy wrapper she'd taken from Melanie and Robby Tuesday morning.

She'd forgotten to throw them out. Hope was about to slide open the matchbox to flush the matches down the toilet when the name of the club on the matchbox captured her attention: the Pelican Inn, Trinidad.

Hope froze. Wasn't Trinidad in the Caribbean somewhere? Melanie and Robby had found the items in the space between the garden shed and the fence that bordered the McClure property. Had someone been hiding there, spying on the house? Hope reached for her cell phone. She had the terrible feeling that whoever had dropped the matchbox and the candy wrapper wasn't a journalist looking for a story.

THE DEEP TIMBRE of Quinn's voice in her ear when he answered his office line on the second ring brought Hope a giddy sense of relief tingling from her fingers to her toes, even though she knew someone would have contacted her if something had happened to him.

"So, you're still alive," she said more sharply than she had intended.

"Good afternoon," he said back smoothly. "How are Kyle and Mel?"

"They miss you and they want to know when you're coming back."

"I wish I had an answer for them."

Hope heard the underlying current of pain in his voice and suddenly felt ashamed for being so hard on him. "I'm sorry, I didn't mean..." Her voice trailed off.

"No, I should have called. I just didn't know what to say, so I chose not to make contact."

Hope's eyes grew suddenly moist. How could she be angry with him when he was being so honest? His honesty rankled a part of her heart that still hadn't recovered from the last time he'd chosen not to contact her but she told herself that Quinn wouldn't leave her again. Wouldn't leave the children. Not by choice anyway.

"Just the sound of your voice would be reassuring," she said with resolute firmness.

"Can I talk to them now?"

"Yes, but I need to tell you something first." She launched into a quick explanation about the matchbox and the cellophane candy wrapper and how Melanie and Robby had found them in Brady's backyard. "The matchbox is from a place called the Pelican Inn in Trinidad."

She heard Quinn's sharp intake of breath. "Have you heard of it?"

"Of course. It's a world-famous watering hole and meeting place. If you want to find a businessman in the afternoon in Trinidad, he'll be in a meeting at the Pelican Inn. Could be that's where the hit was arranged."

"So someone in the Caribbean—like Dr. Chavez or Ross Linville—could have met the hit man there?" she asked.

"Exactly. Chavez resides in the Dominican Republic, but there are a lot of inter-island flights. In fact, I heard from a contact that the doctor went away for a day a couple of weeks ago to an unknown destination. I doubt the Asian crime syndicate would make arrangements for a hit in Trinidad, but I'll keep digging through the information I've been receiving on Adrian Burkhold and the members of Hugh Simons's Payday Ring for any links to Trinidad or the

Caribbean. Where are the matchbox and the candy wrapper now?"

"Here in the room with me. They're on the dresser."

"Can you try to push them into a plastic bag without handling them further? Then put them in a small box. I'll make arrangements with Thacker to have someone meet you to collect the evidence, so stay put until you hear from me again. The lab might be able to get some fingerprints off the matchbox or the candy wrapper."

"But I've touched them and Robby and Melanie have handled them," she protested, worried she may have wiped away valuable fingerprints by shoving them in her pocket.

Quinn chuckled softly in her ear. It sounded deliciously like a caress. "Don't underestimate the wonders of forensic science. We might get a partial print. Thacker called this morning to tell me what the lab learned from the bootprint they found in Quent and Carrie's house. The lab discovered carpet fibers from the chapel and one of those confetti hearts you gave Mel to sprinkle at our wedding imbedded in the print. That's strong corroborative evidence that the person who killed Mr. Drake was the same person who attacked me in Quent's house."

"That's wonderful," she breathed.

"It's a start. Something we can use to build a solid case. Maybe they'll find something in the evidence they collected at your house to help us further identify him. Thacker won't have the lab results until later in the afternoon."

"You'll call me when you get them?"

His hesitation was obvious, and she thought for a moment he wasn't going to give her any more promises.

"I'll let you know as soon as I can. There's one other thing," he said somberly. "I wasn't going to tell you this because I didn't want you to worry, but I got a call this morning that was suspicious." She listened aghast as he gave her the details. "He had ID—probably fake—and paid cash for the room. The maid says he never used the room. Thacker finally got hold of the real Lapointe in Vancouver at the Pan Pacific Hotel."

"But why would the hit man do that?" Hope asked, gripping the phone so tightly her knuckles showed white.

"It could have been a test—I don't know. Maybe he figured out I had a team of people around me and got spooked. Maybe he's just playing mind games— some sickos get off on that kind of thing. Now let me talk to the kids."

Despite her fear, Hope felt a tiny glow light her up from the inside as she tapped Melanie on the shoulder and told her Uncle Quinn was calling. Quinn was strong and smart. They *had* outwitted the hit man so far. Maybe there was hope for them yet.

In the end, Hope loaded the kids in the minivan and spent the afternoon driving up to Carleton Place where Quinn had arranged for her to meet Detective Beauchamp at a doughnut shop. Beauchamp's tweed jacket made him easy to spot. As she drew nearer, ushering Kyle and Melanie toward the detective's table, she noticed he'd ordered doughnut holes and juice for the children and coffee and a raspberry jelly doughnut for her. There was even a high chair drawn up for Kyle.

Hope thanked him for his foresight as she set the diaper bag on a chair and helped the children off with their mittens, hats and coats. Easter might be only a few days away, but it still felt like winter outside.

"No trouble," the detective said, brushing powdered sugar from the front of his tweed jacket as he rose to assist her. When they were all settled and Melanie and Kyle were happily digging into a small box of doughnut holes, Hope unzipped the diaper bag and removed a used and somewhat squashed children's meal box from a fast-food restaurant.

"Sorry about the box, but it was all I could find," she said apologetically.

Detective Beauchamp's brown eyes twinkled in his world-weary face as he opened the box and inspected the contents. "This does the trick. Now, I'd like to hear in your own words exactly where you found these items."

He took notes in a black notebook he withdrew from his pocket, prodding her with a question or two as she described how she'd found Melanie and Robby playing with the matches. "Someone hidden in that spot would have had an unrestricted view of the McClure house," she explained.

Melanie added her own comments about bunny burrows and carrots which the detective responded to with the utmost seriousness. Kyle, having finished his doughnut holes, simply wanted to repossess the hamburger box.

"How long will it take the lab to lift any fingerprints and identify who they belong to?'' Hope asked, breaking off a piece of her doughnut to appease Kyle.

"We should have some results back from the Canadian fingerprint identification system tomorrow. If there's no record, it'll take longer to run them through the FBI and Interpol. Just remember, fingerprints can only identify individuals whose prints are already on file in the system—mostly people who've been arrested or had some reason to be fingerprinted for employment purposes.''

Hope suspected Beauchamp was warning her not to get her expectations too high. "When I spoke to Quinn earlier, he said you were still waiting for the lab results on evidence gathered at my house. Did the lab find anything?'' She took a sip of her coffee.

"Only clothing fibers that caught on the glass when he climbed through the window. He was probably wearing black wool-blend pants.''

Hope tried to hide her disappointment as Melanie climbed into her lap. Hope circled an arm around the little girl's waist, dropped an affectionate kiss on her silky head and prudently moved her cup of coffee out of spilling range. "Quinn thought the matchbox might imply that Ross Linville or Dr. Chavez arranged the hit at the Pelican Inn in Trinidad. What do you think?''

"I think speculation is a necessary element of good police work, and I try never to narrow my options too soon. We could discover that the matchbox in question was picked up by a journalist who'd recently been to Trinidad on a story or on vacation.'' He rose and slipped his arms into the sleeves of a black trench coat. "We'll see what the lab has to say and draw our conclusions from the results."

As Hope watched him leave with the hamburger box in hand, she found herself wondering whether they were about to go one step forward or two steps back.

MERCY WAS ANNOYED with the morning's events. He didn't like deviations in his plans, and he was beginning to suspect that McClure and his partner thought they could outsmart him.

Mercy would teach them a lesson in contingency planning.

Reaching for his cell phone, he punched out a number.

The voice that answered was far too arrogant.

"Did you think you could hide her from me?" Mercy said in a mild, contemptuous tone. "Play your games?"

"I don't know what you're talking about."

"You've been less than truthful with me." His voice lowered suggestively. "And that can be very dangerous."

"McClure doesn't tell me everything."

"How unfortunate for you. You know, I haven't killed a child in months. They are so vulnerable, don't you agree?" Slowly, deliberately, Mercy recited an address. It garnered the reaction he'd anticipated: cold, dead, silence. Complete capitulation.

"Wh-what do you want from me?"

Mercy told him.

A few minutes later he hung up the phone, smiling. The odds were back in his favor.

QUINN MADE A POINT of calling Hope back in the early evening to discuss the other lab results and wish the kids good-night. He felt strange making the call. He couldn't remember his father doing such a thing when he was younger. But then, maybe his father had felt as awkward about the whole business as Quinn did. It was an unsettling thought.

"Daddy!" Kyle's gleeful shout into the phone made Quinn instantly glad he'd called. But he felt a sharp stab of pain that Kyle would never remember Quent. He tried to interpret Kyle's jumbled words to no avail and made appropriate listening noises. "That's great, buddy. Good night. Take good care of the animals in your cage."

Melanie was much easier to understand—as was her tale about the nice policeman who bought her and Kyle and Hope doughnuts. His niece's tiny, forlorn voice brought out his protective instincts in full. "You've been gone so-o long, Uncle Quinn."

Quinn quite agreed. A day and a half and the time stretched like forever. Easter was three days away. He wanted Mel to be thinking about Easter baskets and chocolates. "I miss you, too, sweetheart. Give me a kiss and go to bed nicely for Hope."

Melanie made a sweet kissing sound that made Quinn feel richer than Donald Trump.

He kissed her right back. "That's my girl. I'm glad you had a good day."

"Bye, Uncle Quinn."

"Hi, Uncle Quinn, it's my turn." Hope's voice was softer, with a seductive warmth that quietly stole into every pore of him with the warmth of the sun's rays on a golden summer's day. A soft voice for an incredibly strong woman.

"I'm reporting in with the lab results, as promised."

"I already know about the clothing fibers. I asked Detective Beauchamp at our meeting. He didn't act as if it were earth-shattering news. He wasn't overly optimistic about the fibers or the matchbox and the candy wrapper."

"Those clothing fibers may not seem like much now, but in the long run they might prove helpful. I can't believe I have to give the Reverend Fancy's daughter a lecture about hope."

Hope gave a dismissive snort. "And when was the last time you were in a church?"

"At Kyle's christening. Quent and Carrie took the children to services regularly." Quinn glanced down at a copy of the press release he and Thacker had prepared for the media. It would hit the late evening news tonight. By tomorrow, it would be plastered all over newspapers, and it would be repeated on news broadcasts over the weekend. "In fact, their memorial service will be in their church in Gloucester on Tuesday morning. I just finished making the arrangements. I wanted you to know about it before you saw it on the news."

"I see."

Quinn tried to read her silence.

"And are you hoping their killer will make an appearance?" she asked after a moment.

"That's the plan, but after what happened this morning I'm not so sure. Thacker and I are hoping he won't be able to resist the challenge of it. Thacker will have undercover men posted at the church over the weekend with their eyes peeled for anyone who appears to be checking out the place. If they nab someone, those clothing fibers you so readily dismissed could help put him in prison for a very long time.''

''From your lips to God's ears,'' Hope said softly. ''I have to go now. Kyle's pulled off his clothes and wants his bath, and Mel wants to pour the bubble bath herself. Kyle reminds me of you, the way he's always taking off his clothes. It must be in the genes.''

She hung up before he could give her a silky retort that would make her blush to her roots. He was smiling as he hung up the phone. A small rap on the door frame caused him to lift his head. Oliver was hovering in the doorway.

Quinn had the disturbing feeling that his partner's piercing gaze could decipher his thoughts as if they were written out in ink.

Oliver cleared his throat. ''The arrangements are all made for Tuesday. Why don't you go be with Hope and the kids until then? I have a car standing by for you.''

Quinn leaned back in his chair, his jaw set like concrete. The idea of being in Hope's arms again, in her bed, made his blood boil and his thoughts cloud with steamy images of making love to her. He could show her just how inventive he could be about removing clothes. ''I appreciate the offer, but it's too dangerous.''

Oliver harrumphed as if he couldn't believe his ears. ''Since when has that ever stopped you?''

Since he'd fallen in love with a woman who would, by rights, be another man's wife if he hadn't interfered in her life.

By MID-AFTERNOON on Good Friday, the bed-and-breakfast was filled to capacity with guests for the Easter long weekend. Hope had spent an hour on the phone last night with her friend Jolie, who had cheerfully agreed to look after Hope's regular charges in her own home until their parents had time to make other child-care arrangements. Hope knew the excuse she gave Jolie of a family emergency sounded weak, but at least she wasn't leaving her clients completely in the lurch. The parents knew and trusted Jolie.

Hope tried not to think about how long it might be before she slept beneath the roof of her home again. But having Kyle, Melanie and Quinn in her life was a joy she held tightly to her heart like a closely guarded secret. She did wish she could be with her own family on Easter. Holidays were special occasions in her family. Yesterday, after meeting with Detective Beauchamp, she'd stopped to buy the children some special Easter treats. Saturday night, after they were asleep, she'd fill some plastic eggs with marshmallow chicks and jelly beans in preparation for an egg hunt in their room on Sunday morning.

With the bed-and-breakfast so full, there were lots of children for Kyle and Melanie to interact with in the playroom on the sunporch. Hope was grateful to sit and chat with the other parents supervising their children—though one father had his dark head buried behind a newspaper. Something about the man unsettled her. Would Quinn be that kind of father—too busy to put down his newspaper and watch the children? Too busy to share in their lives?

The man seemed to sense her looking at him, for he glanced up over the edge of the paper and gave her a faint, amused smile that didn't touch the depths of his sea-green eyes. His angular features had a European definition. Hope wondered if he thought she found him attractive and quickly looked away. There wasn't a man on earth who could hold a candle to Quinn.

The mere thought of Quinn made her flush with the remembered heat of their lovemaking.

He hadn't phoned yet today, which probably meant he was still awaiting word on the fingerprints. Hope put her worries on hold as Melanie brought her a tray bearing a cup and saucer of invisible tea and plastic chocolate chip cookies. "Is that for me, lamb?"

Melanie smiled shyly, her brown eyes glowing as she set the tray on Hope's lap.

"How lovely!" Hope told herself that no matter what happened, Melanie and Kyle were going to have happy lives after the tragic losses they'd suffered. "But where is your cup? Tea tastes so much better when you share it with someone."

"I'll get one." Melanie scampered away and came back with a second teacup and saucer. "Know what, Hope?" she said in a conspiratorial whisper as she spooned imaginary sugar into Hope's cup.

Hope leaned forward and whispered back, "What, lamb?"

"I love you."

Hope stroked Melanie's angel curls and added a couple of tears to her cup of tea. "I love you, too."

At dinner, Hope noticed the man again. He sat alone at a table for two across the cheerfully lit dining room, coldly elegant in a black jacket over a black turtleneck. She thought it odd that he was dining alone. Where were his wife and the child or children he'd supposedly been supervising in the playroom? Had they had other plans or were they late in joining him?

She picked at her garden salad, sharing the cucumber and carrot slices with the children, and considered her options for tomorrow. The forecast was calling for sunshine in the afternoon with mild temperatures. They could try the chocolate factory if it was open, or the Rideau Canal Museum. Maybe she could buy a plastic sled and find a small hill for tobogganing. At the very least, the sled would come in handy for taking walks with the children.

Her cell phone beeped as she was leading the children upstairs to their suite. Her heart beat more rapidly, spilling anticipation through her veins the moment she heard Quinn's voice.

"I couldn't wait till bedtime," he murmured silkily. "Thacker just called about the fingerprints."

"And? Don't keep me in suspense," she said impatiently, trying to jam her room key in the lock. The door opened easily. Was it her imagination or had the door not been locked? She dismissed the thought as soon as she stepped into the room and saw everything was just as she'd left it. Marion or one of the maids must have come in to change the towels or restock the toiletries.

"They picked some partial prints off the matchbox that aren't yours or a child's. Unfortunately, there's no record of them in the Canadian system. They're running them through the FBI, France, the U.K. and Interpol. It could be days or weeks until we have a reply. Interpol will send the latent print to various European countries to have it checked in their data bases, but some countries' fingerprint systems aren't compatible with ours and the fingerprints have to be checked physically."

Hope sighed. Were the matchbox and the candy wrapping leads or red herrings? "I suppose you're going to give me another lecture about hope."

"Do I need to?"

How could he sound so wonderfully sexy when he teased her? "No, my life is in your hands."

"I'd settle for having your body in my hands right now. My eyes are glazed over from reading and analyzing background reports. I know more about Adrian Burkhold's life than his own mother, which has led me to the conclusion that he's smart enough to cover his tracks if he's the one who ordered the hit. The private investigator I hired in British Columbia faxed me some information he'd dug up on members of the Payday Ring, though the information on Hugh Simons is a bit sketchy. I also touched base with my contact in the Dominican Republic. He's checked the airlines, and Dr. Chavez didn't buy a ticket to Trinidad or anywhere else in the last two weeks. It doesn't mean he couldn't have chartered a flight, though. And, in case you're wondering, Ross Linville still hasn't surfaced."

Hope's lips twisted in a wry smile at his thorough report. "You didn't mention the Asian Syndicate."

"You can consider them the dangerous unknown quantity. How was your day?"

She told him. She wondered if it sounded boring to his ears. Was she fooling herself into thinking their marriage could work if given the chance?

Hope didn't want to examine the thought too closely.

But it was hovering in the forefront of her mind when she awoke the next morning. She let the children snuggle into bed with her to watch cartoons for a half hour. Then they all washed and dressed for breakfast and Hope carefully packed their bags.

After they'd eaten, they put on jackets, hats and mittens and made their ritual trek out to the barn to visit the animals. Hope's nose tickled at the smell of the alfalfa. Kyle and Melanie never seemed to tire of racing from one pen to the next. She had her hands full keeping the children's excitement under control so they didn't fall and hurt themselves or accidentally pet too hard. Still, Kyle collided with a pair of masculine legs in his haste to see the newborn lambs.

The owner of the legs grabbed Kyle before he fell down from the force of the impact. "Careful!"

Hope recognized the man from yesterday in the playroom. "I'm terribly sorry. He's just very excited."

"I enjoy watching the animals myself." Before Hope could protest, he lifted Kyle in his arms to give him a better view into the sheep pen. "Look at the lambs. Innocent as my young friend here. I'm James, by the way."

Hope lif... Melanie onto her hip so she could have the same view of the lambs as Kyle. "Pleased to meet you. Are you here with your family?"

"I'm awaiting my family. My wife and son were supposed to meet me yesterday, but my wife was detained by her office. I'm hoping they'll be joining me for lunch. Are you enjoying your stay?"

"Very much. The children love the animals and there's lots to visit in Smiths Falls." Hope chatted amiably with James, telling him what they'd already seen and her plans for the day as they toured the rest of the pens.

"Well, thank you very much for keeping me company," he told her as they entered the warm foyer of the bed and breakfast and sat down on the bench provided to remove their boots. He reached into his coat pocket and extracted a handful of candies wrapped in gold cellophane. "Would the children like a butterscotch candy?"

Hope stared down at his offering in instant recognition. "Th-thank you, no," she stammered, trying not to show the fear that split her soul like a jagged bolt of lightning. Surely if this man was truly a father he'd know Kyle and Melanie were too young to eat hard candies? "We just finished breakfast. It was very nice meeting you, too. I hope your family arrives soon." She met his eyes briefly as she smiled, trying to gauge whether a genuine or imagined threat lurked in those sea-green depths. Hadn't she read somewhere that killers and rapists looked like ordinary men? "Come on, children," she said brightly. "Let's get Kyle's diaper changed before the trip to the museum."

Her heart hammered as she led the children toward the stairs. Was it her overactive imagination or could she feel James's gaze on her back? She wouldn't let herself look over her shoulder out of fear of giving her suspicions away.

It was only when she pushed the key in the lock that she remembered finding the door unlocked the night before. Could he have been in her room? Perhaps have planted some kind of listening device? Hope trembled at the thought and quickly ushered the children inside. Thank God she'd followed Quinn's instructions and packed their bags every morning. Trying to move as quietly as possible, she engaged the chain lock, then turned the TV on to make extra noise. As an added measure, she stepped into the bathroom and started the shower running before dialing Quinn's number on her cell phone.

She didn't realize how terrified she was until she heard the familiar gruffness of his voice and felt a part of her latch on to the sound like a lifeline.

"I can barely hear you. Why are you whispering?" he demanded.

"Because I'm scared, damn you. I think the hit man is *here* watching me." She quickly described the man she'd met who'd offered them butterscotch candies.

"Did you take any? His fingerprints might be on them."

Hope groaned and slapped her palm to her forehead in frustration. "I didn't think of it!"

"It's okay. Listen, you told him you were going to the museum, right?"

"Yes."

"Okay, get the kids in the car and drive to the museum. Don't take anything with you but what you can cram in the diaper bag. If he *is* watching you, we don't want to make him suspicious. Act calm and relaxed and stay at the museum until I get there. Just remember, he's not after you. I'm the one he wants."

"How very comforting."

"That's my girl, always looking on the bright side."

"Quinn?"

"Yes?"

"Drive fast."

AN ARROW OF SUSPICION thrust into Quinn's heart, its poison tainting his thoughts as he grabbed his jacket and strode toward Oliver's office. How on earth had the hit man known where to find Hope when he'd been so careful? Only two people knew of her hiding spot: himself and Oliver.

Quinn's stomach churned as he considered the possibility that his friend and partner had betrayed him and supplied the hit man with her location. He couldn't deny that Oliver had appeared visibly strained the last few days. And it would explain why Oliver had been encouraging him to leave the investigation to the police and join Hope and the kids.

Quinn knew without a doubt that the hit man wouldn't show up at the memorial services on Tuesday. The phone call Thursday morning from the man claiming to be Yves Lapointe and the rendezvous at the Ambassador Hotel had likely been a test; the hit man didn't like the odds and was stacking the deck in his favor—using Oliver as an ace up his sleeve to send Quinn out to an isolated area where it would be harder for Quinn to have back-up security.

Quinn paused before the open door to Oliver's office to take a deep breath and calm the anger rioting in his blood. His fists clenched and unclenched. How long had his partner been feeding the hit man information? And why? What possible reason could Oliver have to justify putting Hope and the children's lives at risk?

Stay calm. Act natural, Quinn ordered himself as he cleared the threshold. Oliver looked up from the papers he was studying on his desk.

Quinn slung his jacket over his shoulder and struck a pose of nonchalance. "I just got a call from Hope."

Dark circles underscored Oliver's deep-set eyes. "Everything okay?"

Quinn wondered if a guilty conscience was keeping his partner awake at night. He shrugged and worked his Adam's apple. "Relatively okay. But she's finding it difficult handling the kids by herself. I thought I would take your advice and join her until Tuesday morning."

Oliver's gaze darted toward the photo of his daughter that inhabited the corner of his desk. "I understand. Sometimes a father has to do whatever is necessary for his family."

Quinn rocked back on his heels. Oliver was sending him a deliberate message, a message he'd been too obtuse to see until now.

Two days ago Oliver had deliberately looked at the photo just before Quinn had left to meet Lapointe at the café across from the Ambassador Hotel. Oliver had mentioned Tracy and the joys of fatherhood, and he'd said something to Quinn—what was it? Quinn searched his memory banks until the words floated back to him. *"I'm counting on you to live to be my age."*

Those words suddenly took on a whole new meaning. Quinn wondered where Tracy was now. Oliver had made arrangements to ensure she was in a safe place, but what if the hit man had tracked her down and was holding her hostage to ensure Oliver's co-operation?

Was Oliver playing it safe with his daughter's life and counting on him to outsmart the hit man?

"I'll need the car you said you had standing by."

Oliver opened the desk drawer and tossed him a ring containing two keys. "It's the blue sedan in spot number seventeen in the exterior lot down the block."

Quinn caught them easily. "Thanks."

Oliver's gaze grew hooded. "Don't mention it. Those kids will make a decent father out of you yet."

"What makes you think so?"

"It's Saturday and you're cutting out of work. Must be a first."

The jibe rubbed Quinn the wrong way. Decent fathers didn't abandon their children. Deep down he knew he'd thrust the responsibility for Mel and Kyle's care into Hope's hands, just as his father had relied on his mother to raise him and his brother. His lips thinned. "I'll stay in touch."

OLIVER FELT a suffocating tightness bind his chest like a thin cord as the outer office door closed behind Quinn. His heartbeat raced unsteadily as he reached for the phone to alert the security team to this latest development. He might have broken Quinn's trust, but he could no more abandon his partner than he could Tracy. He just prayed they'd both survive.

"We'll give him a five-minute head start, then we'll follow," Oliver told the head of the team. "Pick me up downstairs. I have two other calls to make."

The third call was the hardest.

"Hi Daddy!" His daughter's voice was vibrant and musical—so like her mother's.

"Good, you're home, princess. I thought you'd be sleeping in," he said gruffly.

"I'm up early studying. I have two papers due next week. I'm probably the only student who turns in her homework by courier."

"I know this has been disruptive to your schedule. I got to thinking about that weekend we spent together last October. Remember the doughnut shop you took me to because you said the doughnuts tasted like the ones I bought you when I was in the RCMP?"

"I remember."

Smart girl. Her voice didn't waver. "Well, I just got done calling the shop and I'm sending you a couple dozen doughnuts by courier to fortify you while you're studying. They guaranteed they'd arrive this morning, so don't leave the house."

Tracy laughed. "I promise I won't leave the house, Daddy, though I don't know what I'm going to do with two dozen doughnuts."

"I wanted to surprise you."

"You've succeeded. I'll be waiting for them."

"Call me when they arrive."

"I will, Daddy. Love you."

"Love you, too, princess."

TRACY WELLS set down the phone and stared with unseeing eyes at the text she'd been composing on the screen of her laptop computer. A tremor wracked her body as she deciphered the message her father had just delivered. It had been frightening enough when he'd called her in the middle of the night and sent her to this address in Sudbury. He wouldn't be sending two dozen cops to her doorstep if she wasn't in immediate danger. Was someone watching her now?

She knew better than to sit or stand directly in front of a window, but her fingers itched to close the living-room blinds. Instinct, however, told her to stay put at the round oak dining table and feign working until the police arrived. The doors and windows were securely locked, the security system engaged.

She tapped a few keys on the laptop. The silence of the house settled around her, abrading her nerves like sandpaper as her ears strained to hear the faintest sound. She hoped the police arrived soon.

And then she heard it. A screeching noise that sounded like a fingernail being dragged across a chalkboard or an outdoor tap being wrenched closed. It came from the back of the house.

Seconds later, the security alarm buzzed in warning. Fear bit into Tracy like shards of glass as she leapt to her feet and cast about for a weapon. Someone had penetrated the house and she had no doubt the intruder meant to kill her.

MERCY LAY IN WAIT for Hope in the parking lot, licking his lips like a wolf about to pounce upon a ewe. The heat generated by his thoughts made him impervious to the cold. Nothing would go wrong this time. Bernardo had assured him a few minutes ago that he'd take great pleasure in holding Wells's daughter hostage. McClure would do exactly as he was told.

Mercy crouched behind a truck as Hope trudged past in the parking lot, holding the children by their hands. He heard her voice, gently urging the children to hurry as she stopped beside a burgundy van and opened the side passenger door. *By all means, hurry to your deaths,* Mercy thought smugly, circling toward the van as she lifted the children into the vehicle and climbed in after them to buckle them into their car seats.

It was far too easy to sneak up on her. Mercy enjoyed the dough-white sheen of shock that transformed her features when she turned around and discovered him standing there, a gun trained on her chest.

"Climb into the driver's seat," he ordered bluntly, "or I'll shoot them, starting with the baby."

Chapter Eleven

Hope stared with horror down the barrel of the pistol and into the marblelike glass of James's sea-green eyes. Oh my God. He meant to kill them.

Her chin quivered. "I'll do whatever you want," she stated as calmly as she could. "But let me leave the children here."

He jutted the gun up and pressed the barrel hard into the skin just beneath her jaw. "I strongly suggest you do whatever the hell I tell you to do and keep your suggestions to yourself. Understand?"

Tears stung Hope's eyes. "Y-yes."

He shoved her violently toward the driver's seat. Melanie screamed as Hope's shoulder smacked the edge of the seat. Pain radiated through her shoulder and neck. She thought of lashing out with her foot, trying to kick the gun from his hand, but she had no doubt he'd turn the gun on the children. She glanced out the side window as she scrambled upright, hoping to see someone in the parking lot she could signal for help.

There was no one in sight. Hope pushed her hair out of her face. "Hush, Melanie," she crooned, trying to reassure the children. Kyle's eyes were round with fear. "I'm okay. Everything will be fine."

Melanie twisted in her car seat as if trying to escape. "I want Uncle Quinn!"

James grinned, his smile raising Hope's hackles. The gun hovered at her side as she fumbled to put the keys in the ignition. "You heard the little girl," James said. "Let's get Uncle Quinn. Drive."

QUINN BRIEFLY CONSIDERED stopping at the nearest car rental company to switch cars out of concern that Oliver might have concealed a tracking device on the vehicle, but he figured it wouldn't make much difference when Oliver had probably already informed the hit man he was on his way. Besides, Hope would be waiting for him at the museum and he didn't want her alone and afraid a minute longer than necessary. He nudged the gas pedal to the floor to overtake a rusted station wagon crawling at a snail's pace. As it was, it would take him an hour to cover the distance to Smiths Falls. He could ditch the car there once he was sure Hope and the children were safe.

His cell phone beeped as he was leaving the outskirts of Ottawa. Quinn responded quickly, thinking it was Hope calling to let him know she'd arrived at the museum.

Disappointment settled like a lead weight in his stomach when he realized it was Clive Yates, the P.I. in British Columbia he'd hired to dig in to the backgrounds of the Payday Ring's members.

"You're up early on a Saturday morning."

Yates's sarcasm hummed over the line. "I haven't

been to bed yet, McClure. I showed up at a club last night in Surrey and met Connie Franklin's sister.''

Connie Franklin was Hugh Simons's girlfriend—the woman who'd got herself hired at the companies the ring had ripped off.

"I just got in," Yates heaved with a tired sigh. "But listen, I found out Connie and Hugh Simons have been together eight years. The sister hasn't made a recent trip anywhere—much less out of the country. She works as a cocktail waitress in a dive and I don't think she has the smarts to organize a hit on her sister's behalf, but we got to swapping stories about families and she mentioned that her sister's boyfriend has a half brother who lived in the state of Washington for a while, smuggling stolen cars into the U.S. The police were looking for him so he went to live in Trinidad with some girl he was shacking up with at the time. He'd got her pregnant and she had family there apparently.''

This was the connection Quinn had been hoping for. Hugh Simons could have asked his half brother to organize the hit. Or the half brother could have taken it upon himself to make amends for Hugh's arrest. Quinn just had to find a way to prove it now. "You got any names?''

"Only the half brother's name—Reggie Simons.''

"You do good work, Yates.''

Yates guffawed. "That's why you pay me the big bucks.''

Quinn immediately dialed Thacker's number to pass along this new information. Concern for Tracy's safety kept him from mentioning to the detective Hope's suspicion that the hit man might be staying

at the bed-and-breakfast. He kept the call brief, wanting to keep the line free for Hope's call.

Why hadn't she contacted him yet? She should be
at the museum by now. The words she'd flung at him
when he'd told her he was leaving her and the children at the bed-and-breakfast in Smiths Falls painfully jabbed his heart. *His loss was her gain.* Quinn
thought about his brother and knew instinctively that
Quent would have agreed wholeheartedly with Hope.
He checked the rearview mirror and didn't like the
coward he saw reflected there. Maybe it was time he
became the man his father should have been.

THOUGHTS OF SAVING the children pummeled Hope's
mind as she numbly followed James's directions onto
the highway. She'd never imagined herself capable
of killing anyone, but the desire to prevent this madman from killing Kyle and Melanie flared like a torch
in her breast. Should she steer into oncoming traffic?
She couldn't risk harming anyone else. Driving into
the snow-filled ditches that lined the highway seemed
a safer option, the children were in car seats. But
what if James wasn't incapacitated? What if he shot
them, then shot some innocent passerby who stopped
to help? Could she ram a telephone pole on the passenger side? No, there were none close to the road.
They were on the other side of the ditches.

Maybe she could signal another driver that she
needed help? How? There wasn't that much traffic
on the road. Houses and farms were few and far between. Fields and stark woods stretched out on the
north side of the highway, while the ice-encrusted
Rideau Canal narrowed and widened in a chain of

lakes, rivers and canal cuts to the south. Merrickville, the next town, wasn't too far. Maybe she could signal someone or ram something once they reached it.

But they didn't stay on the highway long before James ordered her to turn onto a side road toward the canal. The road had been plowed. "Pull over here," he demanded.

Hope's heart wedged in her throat as she pressed on the brakes and brought the vehicle to a halt on the narrow shoulder. There was no traffic on the road. Nowhere to run—not that she could run with the children anyway. Would he shoot them and dump their bodies here?

"Take out your cell phone."

She turned toward him, her mouth dry with terror. "Why?"

He struck her in the face with his free hand. "Shut up and do as you're told."

The side of her face throbbed with pain. Hope unzipped the pocket of her waist pack and curled her fingers around her cell phone.

James handed her a piece of paper with directions written on it. "Call McClure and tell him you were out for a drive—sightseeing along the canal—and you're having car trouble. Say that you turned onto Rideau River Road and pulled into the Montague boat access area on the river. Tell him you want him to meet you." He gripped her chin hard between his thumb and forefinger. She could feel the bruises forming under the cruel pressure of his fingers. "Make it sound convincing or I'll break one of the children's arms."

Hope told herself she wasn't going to cry. She

wasn't going to beg for their lives or show this bastard one iota of the terror consuming her. If he wanted Quinn to come, then they still had a chance of surviving. She had to think, warn him somehow of the trap being laid for him.

"Dial, bitch."

She punched in numbers, her fingers brittle and cold as icicles.

"McClure."

The sound of his name held her terror at bay and filled her with renewed strength. She knew with every fiber of her being that Quinn would do everything possible to save them.

HOPE'S VOICE leapt into Quinn's ear, rattling off words like a runaway train. "Thank heavens I reached you. I'm with the kids in the car—I thought it would be fun to drive along the canal, and hopefully, the kids would doze off for a nap—and we're stuck in the middle of nowhere."

Drive along the canal? Quinn knew instantly something was wrong.

"I think there's a problem with the battery or maybe the ignition," Hope went on. "The engine won't turn over. I wasn't sure about calling a tow truck with the car not being ours and all. Can you come right away? Since I was hoping the kids would fall asleep, I didn't bring any snacks with me. I thought I had some of that *bunny candy* Melanie loves in my purse, but all I found were empty *wrappers.*"

Bunny candy wrappers? Quinn was at a total loss as to what Hope was babbling about. Then he remembered the candy wrappers Melanie had found with the matchbox when she was playing bunnies. He couldn't breathe. Every muscle in his body grew taut. Was Hope telling him the hit man had taken her and the children hostage?

He forced himself to draw in another breath. Was the hit man listening in on the call? "I'm on my way," he assured her. "What road are you on?"

She gave him directions, the strain in her voice causing him to press the gas pedal even closer to the floor.

"I should be there in under an hour." He'd be there in thirty minutes, but the hit man didn't have to know that. "Can you *survive* that long?"

The pause on the other end of the line made him crazy with anxiety. "I—I hope so," she said finally. Bravely.

Quinn's stomach dropped. The words he'd been holding back for a decade rushed to his mouth on a wave of admiration and the fear that he'd never have a chance to say them again. "I love you."

There was no answer. Quinn realized they'd been disconnected.

HOPE FELT as if James were ripping out a piece of her heart when he grabbed the phone from her and turned it off, shoving it into his coat pocket.

Hope stared down at the empty spot in her waist pack where the phone had been. Her gaze fell on her wallet. She still had several thousand dollars cash in it. Maybe he'd accept it as a down payment. "I have money. I can pay you more than the person who hired you—"

"That's doubtful."

"How much?"

"You don't put a price on a man's reputation. Now start the car."

Hope started the car. "Who hired you?"

His fist collided with her temple. "You don't learn quick, do you?"

Hope saw stars as she sagged into the driver's seat.

She told herself she couldn't lose consciousness. Quinn was coming. She had to hold on. It took all her concentration to put the car in gear and pull back onto the road. She didn't even want to think what would happen to them when they reached the canal.

TRACY HEARD a thump like feet landing on the wooden floor—over the warning buzz of the alarm system. Had someone come in through the window? She backed into the kitchen and reached for the heavy marble rolling pin that rested in a holder on the counter. Heart thumping in her chest, she silently moved back into the dining room and headed toward the front door.

She was throwing the dead bolt lock when a male voice stopped her in her tracks.

"Move and I'll blow your brains out, blondie."

Tracy froze, trembling.

"Turn around."

She slowly pivoted, keeping the rolling pin behind her back. A thin man dressed in black from head to toe was pointing a gun at her. Dark eyes bored at her from beneath the concealing thickness of a black ski mask. The warning buzz of the alarm filled her ears, sounding like a flat line on a heart monitor. Why didn't the alarm start ringing—surely thirty seconds had passed?

"Shut off the alarm, quickly," the man ordered, shouting at her. "If it goes off, I'll make you regret you were ever born."

The key pad for the alarm was on the wall beside the front door. She dutifully punched in the silent distress code. Where were the police? She summoned all her courage as she turned to face him again. "What do you want?"

Instead of answering, his eyes skimmed over her, lingering on her breasts. Tracy felt sick to her stomach and her fingers clenched more tightly around the rolling pin.

"Forget it," she said with every ounce of bravado she could inflect into her voice. "You've just walked into a trap. I'm expecting two dozen police officers to surround the house at any second."

"Am I supposed to believe that?"

Tracy lifted her chin and eyed him coldly. "It's the truth. If you want to be arrested, that's your choice." Tires squealed outside in the street. "Don't say I didn't warn you."

The intruder glanced toward the sidelight windows that framed the door and cursed under his breath. Tracy took that moment to hurl the rolling pin at the hand holding the gun. She didn't wait to see the results, she yanked the door open and flung herself into the shrubbery beside the steps, screaming for help at the top of her lungs. Three Sudbury Regional Police cars and a tactical unit had pulled up to the curb.

Seconds later, shooting started and Tracy felt the sharp pain of a bullet lacerating her flesh.

OLIVER PRAYED for his daughter's safety, checking his watch every few minutes as he studied the Global Positioning System's computerized grid. A black X indicated Quinn was on the highway ahead of them, racing toward Smiths Falls.

Minutes crept by and still there was no word. Just when he thought he was going to climb out of his skin, Tracy called.

"Are you okay, baby?"

"Yes, Daddy." To his terror, she started to cry.

"Tracy?"

"Daddy, he shot me. But he only got me in the arm. I was so scared. Thank God you called and warned me."

His daughter had been shot. Cold fury mingled with the guilt that he'd failed in his duty to protect her.

"They're taking me to the hospital in an ambulance, but I told the police I had to call you."

"Is there a police officer with you?"

"Yes," Tracy gulped.

"Let me talk to him," Oliver said. "I'll meet you at the hospital as soon as I can. Quinn's in danger, too."

Tracy sniffed. "Don't worry about me. I'm okay."

Oliver identified himself to the constable and quickly ascertained that Tracy had a flesh wound in her left arm and would be okay. Her attacker had been killed by the police.

"Any ID on him?"

"No, sir. We're combing the area for a vehicle that fits the keys we found in his pocket. Might get a lead from the vehicle registration."

Oliver hoped so. But they might not have answers soon enough to save Quinn. Oliver punched in Quinn's cell phone number. It was time to tell his partner what was really going on.

"GET OUT of the van. The kids, too."

Hope unbuckled her seat belt and climbed into the first rear passenger seat, taking as much time as she dared to release the children from their car seats, Melanie first, then Kyle. Kyle refused to let go of his Blue Baboon, so Hope let him keep it. James had instructed her to drive to the boat access area and park at the end of the road near the canal. She presumed the access was used by ice fishers in the winter since the road was plowed. A gust of cold wind blowing off the river bathed her face as she lifted Melanie to the ground. Hope planted Kyle on her hip and firmly grasped Melanie's mittened hand.

"Walk toward the canal," James ordered.

Hope resisted the impulse to ask why. A vague worry grew in her chest. Here, the Rideau waterway widened to a lake. Pale sunlight glinted off the sprawling icy crust lining its shores. A dull gray patch of water churned in the lake's center, slowly breaking up winter's slick covering with the help of spring's gradually warming temperatures.

Evidence of other footprints and tire treads in the shoulder gave her hope that someone might arrive by chance and throw a wrench in the hit man's plans.

"Here's the way it's going to play," the hit man said smugly. He took a small red rubber ball from his pocket and threw it onto the ice. "You're all going to walk out toward that ball and wait for Uncle

Quinn to join you. If you stop walking, I'll shoot you. Any questions?"

Hope shook her head, not trusting herself to speak. For the life of her, she couldn't understand how some people derived enjoyment from hurting others.

"Get moving."

"Hope, I'm scared," Melanie whined as they stepped onto the ice. "I don't like that man."

"I don't like him either, lamb, but we have to do what he says until Quinn gets here and makes him stop. So hold my hand tight, there's a good girl."

"Will he shoot us?" Melanie asked.

"Not if I can help it." Hope tried to gauge the thickness of the ice by its color as they moved. Near the edge of the lake it was solid white and probably a good foot thick, safe enough to walk on. But far ahead, where the ball lay, the ice had a faint silver sheen which meant it was likely thin and dangerous. Is that what the hit man intended...to send them all crashing through the ice so their deaths looked like an accident?

Hope glanced over her shoulder and saw the hit man moving toward a thicket of trees near the edge of the lake. She stopped. What was he doing?

To her horror, he lifted his gun and fired straight at them. The sound of the shot reverberated in the air. Hope screamed and fell to the ice, dragging Melanie down with her as the bullet dug into the ice ten feet from them. Kyle started to cry.

"Keep moving!" the hit man bellowed at her from the shore.

"Hurry, children." Hope felt a sob rip from her throat as she scrambled to her feet on the slippery ice and lifted Kyle back onto her hip. Melanie clutched her leg. "It's okay, children. Quinn will be here soon. I promise."

Hope prayed it would be true. She didn't dare look backward again, but kept moving forward with the children, hoping the ice would continue to bear their weight.

The ice cracked under her feet like peanut brittle, each step sending a fresh spurt of panic pumping through her heart.

Hope battled her near-hysteria by trying to think of all the things she would require Quinn to do to compensate her for putting her through this terror. He could start by making love to her one hundred days straight. She had a vast collection of lingerie she was sure he would appreciate. He could give her a baby. She wanted to feel her body swell with his baby. Wanted to see his face when their son or daughter entered the world. She wanted to drag him to church and to her family's Easter gathering tomorrow.

She had Easter eggs to decorate and a lifetime of mothering Kyle and Melanie to look forward to. This was *not* going to be the end of things. It couldn't be.

They reached the ball. The ice seemed precariously thin. Hope glanced over her shoulder, scanning the shore. She couldn't see the hit man, but she knew he was hiding somewhere. Joy leapt in her breast when she saw a blue car pull up in front of her van. She hugged Kyle tightly. "There's a car. It's probably Quinn, children. I told you he'd come." *Quinn.* He leapt from the car and she saw the gun in his hands as he braced his arms on the roof of the vehicle. For all his faults and their differences, she'd never loved him more than she did at this moment. "Look out, Quinn, he's in the woods with a gun!" she screamed.

Melanie jumped up and down, waving her arms over her head. "Uncle Quinn! Uncle Quinn, we're here." The ice gave an ominous crackle that sounded like branches being snapped from a tree.

Hope bit back a cry of alarm. Water was seeping up through a fissure not far from where they stood.

QUINN HOPED Oliver wasn't far behind him as he sized up the situation and scanned the woods for signs of movement.

A man's voice rang out from a thicket near the water's edge. "McClure, it's about time you joined us. Throw your gun in the water and head out on the ice toward your family or I'll blow their brains out."

Quinn walked around the car, granting the hit man a larger target. "I have a better idea. Shoot me here and leave them out of this. My keys are in the car."

Laughter echoed from the woods. "That wouldn't be nearly as entertaining." Two shots rang out, followed by screams that brought Quinn to the brink of rage. Blue Baboon arced through the air as though torn from Kyle's hand by a bullet as Hope and the children fell prostrate on the ice. Hope covered the children with her body. Fear that one of them had been hit clamped his heart.

"Enough!" Quinn threw his Glock out toward the open water. It landed on a mirror-thin coating of ice and smashed through with a plop. "I'm playing by your rules."

The hit man was obviously trying to make their deaths look like an accident. Quinn hoped he'd be satisfied to see him plunge through the ice and that the security team would arrive in time to save Hope and the children.

He grabbed a long branch lying on the shore and stepped onto the ice.

"Be careful, Quinn. The ice is thin!" Hope screamed.

"Stay down," he called back. "It'll lessen your chances of falling through."

He hadn't progressed far when the ice began to fracture, cracks streaking out like cobwebs from his feet. Quinn dropped to his belly and crawled toward Hope and the children, keeping the branch horizontal on the ice in front of him. If he fell through, he could grab it and pull himself up.

Behind him, he heard a tremendous thwack, like bucks butting horns. Twisting his head around, he saw a man on the ice, stamping hard, encouraging the section Quinn was on to break off.

He also saw Oliver and three other men, sneaking up on the man from behind.

Quinn tried to keep the hit man distracted. He could hear Hope shushing the children. "So now you're coming out in the open, you bastard. Does it make you feel like a man to kill defenseless people in their sleep—hiding in the dark and in the bushes? You're a real tough guy. Put down the gun and come out here. We'll see who's tough."

The hit man circled ten paces to his right. "That's the problem with you cops. You want to control situations with your brawn instead of your brains. Why don't you beg, McClure? Beg me for mercy to save your wife and your niece and nephew. I wonder which one you'll try to save first if they all go into the water." He raised his right leg and brought it down hard.

Another resounding thwack rent the air.

Just behind Quinn a chunk of ice the size of a pitcher's mound broke free and wobbled like an ill-fitting puzzle piece in its hole, water slipping over its surface. Quinn glared at the hired killer. "Go to hell. And take Hugh Simons with you. While you're at it, take his brother Reggie, too, and make it a three-some."

The hit man smiled, neither confirming nor denying that Simons had hired him. He raised his leg again. "Save me a spot, McClure."

Quinn wanted to bury his fist in those even white teeth. A few more meters and Oliver and the others would be within striking range. "What makes you think I'll get there before you do? You're the idiot jumping on thin ice."

As the hit man opened his mouth to retaliate, Oliver tackled him, the force of their impact sending tremors through the ice. The security team was on them instantly, disarming the hit man. Quinn derived a real sense of satisfaction from hearing fists and boots pound into the hit man's flesh while they cuffed him.

Quinn started crawling toward Hope, relief burgeoning through him. Catching his brother and sister-in-law's killer wouldn't bring them back, but their memory would live on in Kyle and Mel and the world would be a little safer. A world he planned to share with Hope if she would still have him. "We got him, sweetheart. Stay right there."

"Oh, Quinn!" The answering golden glow in her

eyes warmed his soul. Nothing seemed more important to him than reaching her, holding her in his arms. She'd been so brave. But there was a good fifteen meters of precariously thin ice stretching between them.

He shouted for Oliver to get someone to check the cars for some ropes and call for help.

"We're on it, Quinn," Oliver hollered back.

Quinn inched forward a couple more meters. To his despair, he realized it was too unsafe to attempt to go any farther. His added weight might send them all to a watery grave. He thrust the branch toward them. "I don't think I can come any closer. Melanie, crawl towards me and grab the stick."

"How come I have to hold the stick, Uncle Quinn?" his niece asked.

Quinn didn't want to frighten her further by pointing out the danger they were still in. Water was oozing up through the cracks all around them. "It's a game, sweetie. I might have to pull you. Crawl on your hands and knees."

Hope shifted, giving Melanie an encouraging pat. To Quinn's horror, Kyle suddenly wormed free of Hope's grasp and toddled toward his Blue Baboon. "Mine," he said, his chin jutted out stubbornly.

"Kyle, no!" Hope stretched out an arm, trying to snag him.

With a chortle, Kyle eluded her grasp, determined to retrieve his friend. As he bent to pick up his toy, the ice gave way beneath him. Kyle sank into the water with a startled cry.

Hope made a desperate lunge toward him, trying to save him. Quinn's heart shattered as the ice parted and swallowed her, too.

Chapter Twelve

The shock of sliding into the frigid water nearly knocked Hope unconscious. The current pulled at her, and she tried to kick, but her body felt numb. She could hardly move her legs. She had to find Kyle. Where was he?

She saw a movement. The neon-yellow stripe on his jacket. Lungs burning, she clamped her arms around her baby, jabbing one of his legs beneath the strap of her waist pack, so they couldn't be separated. She couldn't think, couldn't move. She only hoped the current would bring them toward the light.

QUINN WATCHED the spot where Hope and Kyle had fallen in, praying to see them surface, torn between the instinct to dive frantically after them and the need to help Melanie, who was screaming hysterically.

It seemed to take forever to coax his niece to keep moving toward him. When he finally had his hands on her, he grabbed her to him, kissed her cheek and told her she had to be a big brave girl and keep crawling toward Oliver, who was approaching with a rope and two other members of the security team.

Oliver threw the rope toward Quinn. It landed short, and Quinn wasted more precious time scooting to reach it. How long could Hope and Kyle survive in the water? He tied the rope around his waist, his numb fingers seeming to move too slowly. The knot finally secure, he grabbed the branch and slid on his belly toward the area where Hope and Kyle had disappeared. Could the current have carried them downstream beneath the ice?

Quinn heard a shout behind him. One of the security team members was pointing to a watery area twenty to thirty meters downstream. Quinn saw something bobbing in the water. God, was it Blue Baboon?

Quinn slithered toward the hole like a madman. He flicked the toy out of the water with the stick and onto the ice. Then he used the stick to pry up wafers of ice around the edges of the hole, enlarging it. Like a gift from heaven, he saw a ribbon of dark silk, then Hope slipped up from under the ice, her hair floating around her head. He called out to Oliver and snagged her with the stick. To his relief he saw Kyle's body tangled with hers. Quinn grabbed Hope's leg and shouted to Oliver and the other men to pull.

Time seemed frozen as Hope's and Kyle's bodies were dragged to shore. The rescuers worked to remove their sodden clothes and bundled them in blankets and coats, then started artificial respiration. Kyle had a weak pulse and came round to consciousness for a few brief seconds. Hope had no pulse.

She'd risked so much for him and what had he given her in return?

An ambulance and the Ontario Provincial Police

arrived. Quinn insisted that Blue Baboon accompany Kyle in the ambulance. He didn't remember anything about getting to the hospital or even think to ask the police if they'd found ID on the hit man. He didn't care. He held Melanie in his lap, tucked close to his heart, and willed Kyle and Hope to survive. Somehow in the last eight days his world had narrowed and his focus had shifted. Hearing Kyle call him Daddy gave him more inner satisfaction than solving a tough case. He was so grateful to be granted this second chance to have a family. He only hoped a woman with the courage of a platoon of soldiers would give him the chance to remain her husband.

"Is she going to wake up?" Melanie asked, her lower lip quivering, when Quinn held her in front of the window looking into Hope's room in ICU after they'd been allowed to check on Kyle in his hospital room. The doctors had said Kyle was stabilized and was going to be fine, but he would need to be transported to the children's hospital in Ottawa for a few days of observation.

It was Hope that Quinn was worried about now and he shared Melanie's sense of disappointment. He'd been told Hope was breathing on her own and they were warming her slowly with hot packs and warm fluids and monitoring her heart. But he wanted to look into Hope's eyes and be reassured by her smile. "Yes, Hope is going to wake up soon," he assured his niece in a low tone, stroking her back, "but we'll let her rest for now. Maybe she'll be awake after we get something to eat. How would you like to be my date for an early dinner, hmm?"

"Can we go to McDonald's?"

"No, we're going to the hospital's cafeteria."

"Does it have a playground?"

"Probably not, but I'll let you push the buttons in the elevator. And we can look to see if there's a place where we can buy Hope some flowers."

"Good. Mommies and fairies like flowers and Hope's a mommy and a fairy fiancée."

"Whatever you say, cupcake. Let's check the waiting room to see if Oliver's here. Maybe he wants to get something to eat with us."

They found Oliver in the waiting room, along with Hope's family and her ex-fiancé, David Randall. A sudden silence fell upon the room as Quinn entered, and he felt a battalion of accusatory glances trained on him. The Fancy family was nothing if not loyal to their own. Tom Parrish looked decidedly uncomfortable. Hope's three other brothers-in-law eyed Quinn as if they'd like to thrash him.

The Reverend Fancy, a tall man with slightly rounded shoulders, strode toward Quinn, his expression fierce and his mouth drawn into a line of obvious displeasure. "Is it true what Tom says—that you've married my daughter?"

Quinn nodded, not wanting to go into details in front of Melanie or the eight other children listening. "Did Tom explain the extenuating circumstances, sir?"

"Yes, not that I'm any more pleased with his behavior than I am yours. You should be ashamed of yourself for taking advantage of Hope's good nature and preying on her sympathy. As if you haven't hurt her enough already. She could have been killed. And you recklessly put Tom and Faith and my grandchildren at risk. I don't want you anywhere near our family. I've just informed the nurses I don't want you to see my daughter.''

David Randall came to stand beside Hope's father and Quinn wondered what explanation he'd given Hope's family for the bandage on his nose. Randall looked irritatingly arrogant. ''Tom says the marriage can be annulled.''

Quinn wasn't about to broach the topic of David and Hope's broken elopement in this public argument. ''I think that's Hope's decision, don't you? I'll be down in the cafeteria if Hope wakes and wants her husband.''

''Well, they seemed friendly,'' Oliver quipped when they had escaped into the aseptic calm of the corridor.

Quinn laughed, but unease had settled like a burr under his skin. ''About as friendly as a pack of wolves baring their teeth.''

''How come that old man was yelling at you, Uncle Quinn?'' Mel asked, tucking her head into the curve of Quinn's neck.

Quinn hugged her. ''Because daddies get very protective of their little girls. Speaking of which—'' he glanced at his partner, catching Oliver's eye, ''—how's Tracy?''

''She's fine. She's got a few stitches and she's excited because a very cute constable was assigned the task of driving her up to Ottawa. I want to give her a hug before I send her back to school.'' Oliver bowed his silver head. ''I'm sorry I—''

''Don't say it,'' Quinn said as they waited for the

elevator. "Don't be sorry you trusted me. You made all the right decisions. We nabbed him. Do they have any idea who he is?"

"He's got a British Columbia driver's license that says he's James Owens. It's a good fake. Tracy's attacker rented a car using a B.C. driver's license in the name of Bernard Smith. His ID was probably fake, too. His driver's license number is identical to the number on Owens's."

Quinn frowned as a thought flickered in his head. "We need to convince Thacker that it'll be worth his while to pass us copies of those fake IDs. Remember the police seized several boxes of fake IDs when the Payday Ring was arrested? If Owens's and Smith's IDs can be linked to one of the originals in those boxes, it will corroborate that Hugh Simons arranged the hit and his brother in Trinidad acted as the middleman."

"Thacker's case has just expanded to include counterfeiting," Oliver replied. "I think he'll be smart enough to figure out we can get results faster than the RCMP lab. Then he can tell the lab his suspicions and let the lab verify it. By the way, Thacker said he'd run Owens's and Smith's prints ASAP."

Quinn nodded his approval as the elevator doors opened with a ding. But all he could concentrate on at the moment was taking care of Melanie and Kyle and finding a way past Hope's family so he could have the most important conversation of his life with his wife.

THE CLOUDS convinced Hope she must be in heaven. Blessedly, the icy darkness was gone and she was snuggled up to her chin in a fluffy mantle as cozy as a down comforter. Light glowed around her, but she knew her eyes were closed. Someone—an angel?— had taken her by the hand, and Hope's worries fell away. The strong warmth of that guiding hand reassured her she was safe and loved.

And would be always. If only she would open her eyes and face what was ahead.

Her eyelids lifted, and a man materialized in front of her. For a fraction of a second she thought it must be Quentin, meeting her in heaven, but when her gaze locked with the liquid silver simmering in the man's eyes, she knew instinctively it was Quinn. That she wasn't in heaven, but in a hospital bed, and he had somehow saved her.

Quinn's handsome features were gripped with a grim intensity that sent a jolt of alarm piercing the layers of warmth that surrounded her. Something was terribly wrong. Memory came crashing back along with an image of Kyle scrambling out of her grasp after Blue Baboon.

"Kyle?" His name leapt from her lips on a sharp cry. Tears blurred her vision. It was her fault....

Quinn's fingers tightened around hers. "Ssh! Don't upset yourself or the nurse will throw me out. He's fine. They're transferring him to the children's hospital for a few days for observation. But it's only a precaution."

Hope gripped his fingers fiercely. "You wouldn't lie to me, would you?"

"I wouldn't dare."

She sighed, acknowledging that he'd never shied

away from telling her a painful truth. "Please tell me the hit man didn't escape again."

"Not this time. Thanks to Oliver, he was arrested. Thacker and Beauchamp will come to take your statement once your doctor decides you're up to it." He loosened his fingers from her grasp and patted her hands, almost awkwardly. "I promise we'll talk more about it later—and settle a few *other* things—when you're fully recovered. I can't stay long. The doctor didn't want to let me see you at all, but Mel and I are going with Kyle to the children's hospital and I convinced him that Melanie needed to see you awake. She's waiting outside with a nurse, but we had to promise we wouldn't touch you or come within arm's length of the bed." He glanced at the heart monitor hooked up to her. "Your heart's suffered a shock and an accidental bump could be very dangerous in your fragile condition."

Is that why he hadn't kissed her? "You've already broken your promise," she teased.

Quinn abruptly turned away from her, leaving her feeling more confused than ever. If the hit man was under arrest and Kyle would be fine, why didn't Quinn look more jubilant? Was the shock of Carrie's and Quent's deaths setting in now that he was no longer running for his life? There was obviously more going on in Quinn's mind than he was admitting, but for now, the precious few minutes the doctor had allotted them would be better spent reassuring Melanie she was all right. "Will you be okay taking care of Melanie on your own?" she asked him as he crossed to the door.

"Yes. Don't sound so skeptical." He glanced back

at her, his mouth jerking in a crooked smile that made her breath catch. "I've been hanging around an expert and I think I can remember to feed, clothe and keep her entertained. I'm more worried about leaving you here alone than I am about taking care of that little princess." He hesitated, his hand on the door, his eyes studying her. "Will you be okay? Your family's here."

"Oh."

"And David."

"Oh."

"They all know the real reason for our marriage."

Hope winced as her cheeks grew hot with guilt. Oh God, her family.

10:32 a.m. Monday

FOR TWO DAYS, Hope held her family and David at bay. How could she tell them what the future held for her until she and Quinn had had a chance to talk privately?

Detectives Thacker and Beauchamp had been frustratingly uninformative when they'd come to take her statement. They'd mumbled something vague about waiting for lab results and fingerprint checks, which she took to mean they hadn't identified the hit man or his accomplice, or determined who'd hired them. Did that mean the person might take out a second contract on Quinn?

Quinn was just as evasive when she phoned him several times during the weekend for updates on Kyle's condition. Though she'd spoken to Kyle on the phone last night, as soon as she was discharged

Monday morning Hope convinced her mother to drive her directly to the children's hospital so she could see Kyle for herself.

Hope twisted the wedding band Quinn had given her around her finger as they approached Ottawa. The pot of rose-colored hydrangeas Melanie had given her in the hospital was carefully wrapped and tucked into the back seat of her mother's car. She missed the children. And she missed Quinn.

Most of all, she was afraid that he'd been so uncommunicative because he didn't know what to say. Had he changed his mind about their marriage?

"Hope, slow down, I can barely keep up with you," her mother complained after they'd asked for directions to Kyle's room.

But Hope couldn't slow down. A smile grew inside her as she counted the room numbers and finally found Kyle's. "Hello, darling," she sang out as she entered. Melanie gave a cry of surprise, and Hope felt Quinn's gaze on her as she headed toward the bed where Kyle was building a tower with blocks. Kyle's eyes lit up as he stretched out his arms to her, knocking over the blocks.

Hope laughed and started to cry as she gently enfolded him in her arms. "Oh, you little monkey, you. I missed you." His delightful little-boy scent enticed her to plant several kisses on his tousled head. He looked, and felt, perfect.

Hope felt a hand tugging on her coat. "My turn," Melanie demanded.

"Of course! How silly of me." She gave Kyle a last worshipful kiss and dropped to one knee to give Melanie a snuggle.

Then she lifted her gaze to meet Quinn's. He looked worse than he had the other day. A day's worth of stubble coated his jaw and dark circles ringed his eyes. But what worried her more were the dark shadows she saw in his eyes.

"Quinn, what—?"

Her mother's arrival at the door stopped her from asking him what was wrong. "Mom, you remember Quinn."

"How could I forget," her mother said stiffly. "I'm sorry about your loss."

"Thank you, Mrs. Fancy," Quinn said curtly, his fingers winding tightly around the rails of Kyle's bed.

Hope put her hand on Melanie's shoulder and tried to fill the awkward silence with more introductions. Surely her mother wouldn't extend her crisp disapproval toward the children. "This is Melanie...and Kyle."

Melanie tilted her head to one side and stared up at Hope's mother. "You're pretty, like Hope. Are you a fairy fiancée, too?"

Ruth Fancy laughed. "I'm not sure what you mean, but it sounds so delightful I think I would like to be one. Do you children like licorice? I always keep some in my purse for my grandchildren. Hope, why don't you and Quinn go down to the cafeteria for a coffee? I'm sure you have a lot to discuss. I'll stay with the children."

Quinn decided Hope had definitely inherited her directness from her mother. He held the door open for Hope, but he didn't want to go to the cafeteria where they would be surrounded by people. Hope looked so incredibly beautiful. Color bloomed in her cheeks and her eyes shone with fire. She was wearing a new coat with a fur edging around the hood. The bronzed gold fabric of the coat complemented her eyes. Quinn wanted to sink his fingers into the fur and drag her into the nearest utility closet to ravish her with kisses and promises until they were both shaking and weak from pleasuring each other.

To his surprise, she wrapped her fingers in his black sweater and pushed him against the wall of the corridor. "Okay, out with it. You said we needed to talk. Thacker and Beauchamp wouldn't tell me anything about the hit man. I want to know what's going on."

Quinn stared at her in astonishment and with rapidly mounting ardor. He didn't know which was more enticing: the feminine sweetness of her curves hovering inches from him or the damned determination that shone in her eyes. How had he ever been arrogant enough to walk away from everything she'd offered him? His ardor was quenched by the crushing weight of guilt over what he'd put her through. Had his father ever appreciated everything his mother had done for their family? He could see now that his mother had been the glue that gave what they'd had meaning and substance.

"Start talking, McClure."

Quinn quietly told her how the hit man had located Oliver's daughter and threatened her life if Oliver didn't keep him informed as to Quinn's whereabouts.

"Oh my God. How did you guess what was going on?"

His mouth twisted with irony. "Oliver told me in so many words, I just wasn't paying attention. He had a contingency plan in place. Fortunately, it worked."

"Is it true you don't know yet who hired the hit man?"

"I'm afraid so. But we do know his fingerprints match the partial print the lab lifted from the matchbox, and that the bootprint the Ident team found on the dryer in Quent's house was left by the hit man's boot. We should know sometime today whether or not the fibers they found caught in your bedroom window came from his clothes. They found a .22 semiautomatic in a bag in the hit man's car at the bed-and-breakfast that we think he used to kill Quent and Carrie. They're running ballistics tests. We might not be able to identify him yet, but we will eventually."

Quinn cleared the painful lump in his throat. "The suspect's not talking and the man who attacked Tracy is dead. They both were carrying fake ID. But we have a strong lead." He led her toward a pair of chairs in an empty waiting room at the end of the corridor and told her how the private investigator had learned that Hugh Simons had a half brother in Trinidad. "I don't think it's a coincidence that the fake IDs the killers were carrying were from British Columbia." He told her about the boxes of fake IDs that were seized when the Payday Ring was arrested. "I'll be going to British Columbia to check it out— I just hope Simons was stupid enough to have the ID manufactured from his or another Payday Ring member's ID."

"What if you can't find out who hired him? What if the person realizes the hit man failed and hires someone else?'' Hope's voice was so strained, Quinn suspected that she'd had a change of heart over the deal they'd made and decided the cons definitely outweighed the pros.

"I can't guarantee we'll find out who hired him," he admitted, "but the investigation is far from over. We have other options. We have his cell phone." He swallowed hard. "I know this has been very hard for you. You've been incredible. I want you to know that I understand if you want to back out of our arrangement so you can be with David. I can find a nanny to watch the kids until the investigation is finished and I've had a chance to organize my life. Oliver's already been in touch with a nanny agency."

The color drained from her cheeks.

"You don't have to say anything, Hope. I'll never forgive myself for endangering you like that. I want you to have love in your life. I don't want you to sacrifice your dreams for Kyle and Mel. I can take care of them on my own and do all that other stuff single parents do."

"You mean I'm not irreplaceable?"

His finger tilted her chin up. "You are definitely irreplaceable. Now that I've scientifically proven you're no longer jinxed, I think you should marry David and have those babies the two of you talked about."

"Is that so?"

"Yes."

Hope had never been so angry in her life. The dreams she'd been nurturing since he'd reentered her life were burst by his suggestion. Quinn had promised he'd never divorce her, but granting her an option to leave the marriage amounted to an unforgivable act of treason after everything she'd confided in him. Doubts crowded her mind, sabotaging her confidence. Had he made all those promises because he'd never thought he'd survive to keep them? She knew better than anyone that he never would have married her if there hadn't been a gun to his head.

Did she really want to hold him hostage for the rest of their lives? He'd always been honest with her. Was this his way of telling her he didn't love her? Allowing her to save face?

Pride kept her from asking outright as she searched his face for some sign he was being noble. Some indication that his lovemaking was a reflection of his true feelings for her, and not just a pleasant temporary physical release. How could he put her in this position?

The damage was done. Noble or not, she couldn't stay married to a man who wasn't fully committed to their union. No matter how much she loved him.

Her gaze raked his rugged, familiar features. With a sigh, she realized she'd probably always love him with the worshipful, out-of-control passion that a woman saves for her first love. No one expected James Bond to give up his job and become a devoted husband. She had no one to blame but herself for letting herself be swayed by the extraordinary circumstances and the intensity of her attraction for him.

She'd been dumped at the altar by David. Why shouldn't she add an annulment to the list of her broken relationships? With all the courage she could muster, she pulled the wedding band from her finger and held it out to Quinn. Her voice was amazingly serene, but then, she had experience at this sort of thing. "There you go. I'll tell Tom he can start annulment proceedings. But don't worry about finding a nanny for Kyle and Mel. You have enough to deal with. I'll watch them while you go to B.C." Hope straightened her shoulders and put her hand on his. The heat of his skin burned into her. Compassion wouldn't let her abandon the children or him, even if they weren't going to live as man and wife. "The memorial service is tomorrow. Were you planning to take the children with you?"

"No. Kyle's supposed to be released tomorrow morning. I thought I'd pick him up after the services."

"Why don't I pick him up instead? Then you won't have to worry about it. I'll come early so you'll have a chance to go home and change for the funeral. Tomorrow will be hard for you. I could take Melanie home with me now if it would help."

"Are you sure? I don't know how long I'll be away. I thought I'd take the children and the nanny with me. I'd planned to make a brief trip to Halifax first. Carrie's dad is in a nursing home there. I need to tell him what happened."

"Of course I'm sure. The children can stay here with me while you're gone. They know me and they've had enough change in their lives without being dragged across the country and introduced to another caregiver. Besides, I refuse to give them up until we know for certain who hired the hit man and that you're no longer in danger."

"I'm not sure you realize what you're agreeing to," Quinn said. "It could be a week to ten days, maybe longer, to prove the hit man's ID and his accomplice's are counterfeit and to determine the original document they were manufactured from. Simons's pretrial hearing starts a week from Friday and I have to be there to give testimony. That could take a few days. I might not be back for a couple of weeks.''

''That's fine. The children will be okay as long as you call often.''

''I will. I'll pay you—''

''Whatever.'' She dismissed his offer with a shrug. Right now Hope didn't want to think about the sensual cost she'd foolishly hoped to extract from him. Taking care of Kyle and Mel would be a joy.

Quinn slowly put the ring in his pocket and offered her his hand as they walked back down the corridor to Kyle's room.

Hope wondered how long it would take her mother to realize her finger was bare.

Chapter Thirteen

Being away from Hope and the children was far more difficult than Quinn had anticipated. They were never far from his thoughts as he set about the task of proving a connection between the hit man and the Payday Ring.

His first destination was the British Columbia Ministry of the Attorney General where he tracked down some blank driver's licenses from the motor license office that matched the issue of the hit man's and his accomplice's fake IDs. Then he paid a visit to the printer of the blank license forms to confirm exactly what technology was used to produce a genuine driver's license. Pinpointing the differences in printing methods was a critical step in determining whether a document was genuine or counterfeit. His last stop was to the manufacturer of the paper the driver's licenses were printed on, where he obtained a sample of the special paper used.

Now he was ready to begin his analysis—provided the original driver's license that had been used to manufacture both fake licenses could be found in one of the boxes stored in the evidence room.

Determination fueled him as he took the ferry to Nanaimo on Vancouver Island where he met with Corporal Scott, the RCMP officer in charge of the Payday Ring's investigation at the Nanaimo RCMP detachment. Corporal Scott was built like a long-distance runner and had a crooked, reserved smile beneath a sandy pencil-thin mustache.

The corporal extended his hand to Quinn. "McClure, I've been expecting you. Sorry about your brother and his wife. It's a shame."

"Thank you."

"We're all set up in one of the interview rooms. Detective Thacker explained what you'd be looking for and the material has been checked out of the evidence room."

Quinn picked up the cases containing his portable lab and followed Corporal Scott down a hallway. The exhibit person, a uniformed corporal with a ruddy complexion, introduced by Scott as Corporal Wilson, waited for them in the interview room. Corporal Wilson had laid the bagged licenses out on three tables. His watchful presence ensured that Quinn couldn't tamper with the evidence.

Quinn knew exactly what he was looking for as he carefully scanned the licenses. In preparation for trial, the RCMP lab here had already matched the fake licenses to the originals they were counterfeited from. Quinn just had to determine if one of these originals had been used to manufacture the hit man's and his accomplice's IDs.

Using the microscope, he examined the originals for accidentals—telltale signs of retouching, such as a break in the line of a box made when the personalized information was removed from the original license. Three accidentals were evident in the color photocopies he'd been given.

Half an hour later, his lips tightened in satisfaction when he found the right original license. "This is the one you want to send to Ottawa for comparison."

Constable Scott looked up the exhibit number on the license and clapped Quinn on the shoulder. "That's Hugh Simons's license."

"Bingo." The energy drained from Quinn's body. Hugh Simons and the hit man would get what they deserved. But Quent and Carrie were irrevocably gone. Quinn needed a good stiff drink.

THE MORNING Hope had been dreading finally arrived. Quinn had returned from Simons's pretrial hearing late last night and would be picking the children up this morning. Last night she'd packed Kyle's and Mel's things into two duffel bags and carried them down to the foyer where they waited near the door. She'd hidden a gift for each child in the bags. She sat with the children on the couch reading them Kyle's favorite story about a dump-truck driver who gave an assortment of animals slides in the tilting bed of his dump truck. Quinn would be here any minute and Hope didn't know how she was going to say goodbye to these two darlings.

She'd made arrangements for Jolie to watch her other charges today and for the rest of the week. She wanted to go away by herself for a few days to come to terms with her separation from Quinn and the children.

She'd been very careful to evade Quinn's questions about her plans with David. She had no plans for resuming her relationship with David. She was only grateful Quinn seemed blind to the fact she loved him.

He was proving himself to be the father she'd always known he could be. Kyle and Melanie would thrive in his care. He'd phoned every day and had sent gifts and sweets to the children via a courier. He'd also told her the wonderful news that the hit man's fake ID had matched Hugh Simons's original driver's license and that the police had identified the hit man via his cell phone records. His real name was Michael Kolaczek. He'd begun his career as a hired executioner working for a drug lord out of Miami. His accomplice, who'd been shot and killed by the Sudbury police, was Anthony Bernardo. The hit man's cell phone records also seemed to confirm that Reggie Simons had arranged the hit on his brother's behalf. He'd been arrested in Trinidad and was awaiting extradition.

Police authorities all over the world were contacting the Canadian police authorities in hopes of connecting Kolaczek with unsolved professional hits in their countries. Hope shuddered just thinking about the number of people Kolaczek had killed.

She heard Quinn's car as it turned up the drive. Her heart started to pound. Oliver had seen to having the children's belongings moved to Quinn's condo and had hired a live-in nanny. There'd be no reason to see Quinn or the children ever again.

"Uncle Quinn's here, children."

Kyle and Mel jumped off the couch and ran for the front door. Hope hurried after them, urging the children to get their coats from the rack in the closet while she tucked the storybook in Kyle's bag. She didn't want this to take a second longer than necessary.

She was helping Kyle put his boots on when the doorbell rang. Hope opened the door with a smile that was far from genuine. Quinn, blast him, looked more handsome than any man had a right to look. He wore a black leather jacket over a gray sweater and black corduroys. And he was carrying an enormous wrapped box.

She stared suspiciously at the box. It didn't look as harmless as the white fluffy clouds printed on the sky-blue wrapping paper. "What on earth?"

Melanie skipped excitedly. "Is that for me, Uncle Quinn?"

"No, silly goose, it's a present for Hope. To thank her for taking care of you."

"You shouldn't have, Quinn."

"But I did." He stepped into her home, filling the foyer and her heart with his nearness, and set the box on the floor. "Open it."

Hope was grateful for the children's presence. They helped her tear off the paper wrappings, their excited chattering masking her silence. Hope ran her hand over the beautiful tapestry suitcase. A suitcase? She didn't know what to say.

Quinn was looking at her so intently it unnerved her. "It's lovely. Thank you."

"It's for your honeymoon—to keep your undergarments from falling out at awkward moments."

Hope blushed deeply at his reference to her broken suitcase. He pulled a blue envelope from the inner pocket of his jacket. "This is for you, too. Since you wouldn't give me a figure for baby-sitting, I took the liberty of coming up with a payment on my own."

Hope took the envelope from him and laid it on the table to open later. "It really wasn't necessary."

"You're not even going to look at it?"

Was it her imagination or did he seem disappointed? "Not now. I have more important things to do—like kiss these two imps." Hope grabbed Kyle and peppered his plump cheeks with kisses until he roared for her to stop. Then she embraced Melanie, smoothing her angel curls one last time.

This was harder than she had thought it could possibly be. Her chin quivered as she stood up and herded the children toward the door while Quinn grabbed the bags.

She stood on the porch, clinging tightly to a column, her jaw snapped closed, watching Kyle and Melanie hop like toads from puddle to puddle in the yard while Quinn threw the bags in the trunk of a gray luxury sedan.

The weather had warmed since Easter, melting the snow and unveiling yellow stretches of grass. The euphoric taste of spring was in the gentle breeze. Mel and Kyle were happy to be without hats and gloves. Hope laughed despite the crushing pain in her chest as Quinn scooped Melanie from a puddle and deposited her in her car seat, then returned for Kyle. Kyle raced around a drooping forsythia bush fat with buds, his laughter at evading Quinn bringing Hope ever closer to the brink of tears. She clung to the column more tightly. Only another minute or two and she would be alone.

Quinn captured Kyle near the apple tree and hoisted him over his shoulder like a sack of potatoes, carting him to the car. Hope bit the inside of her cheek and counted off the seconds as Quinn buckled Kyle into his car seat. Fifty-three seconds.

Quinn straightened, slamming the rear door. Sunlight glinted off his hair as his gaze slowly lifted to meet hers across the roof of the car. His eyes were warm with friendship and gratitude, maybe even tears. She told herself she'd survived her last parting with him. She'd survive this one. She raised one hand and waved, mouthing goodbye.

His jaw tightened, even from this distance she could see the muscles clench. To her relief he climbed in the car. Hope kept up the pretense of waving as the car started and headed down the drive. When it dipped out of sight at the end of the drive she sank to the porch's peeling floorboards and buried her head in her arms, letting the tears come.

She was sobbing so hard, she didn't hear the car back up or Quinn approach. All she heard was his voice as he called her name. Her head jerked up and she desperately wiped at her cheeks as Quinn strode up the brick path, his expression fierce. Had the children forgotten something?

He pulled his wallet from his pants pocket as he approached. God, he wasn't going to offer her more money, was he? Hope didn't bother standing. He obviously knew she'd been crying, denying it would only make her feel more foolish.

"I'm sorry to disturb you," he said almost contritely, his eyes gleaming as he removed a piece of paper from his wallet and thrust it at her. "I'm looking for this woman. I thought maybe you might know her.''

Hope glanced at the paper and realized it was a photo. Of her—taken at the wedding where they'd met. She recognized the peach dress and the naiveté of her expression. ''She looks vaguely familiar,'' she admitted grudgingly, wondering what he was up to. ''Why are you looking for her?''

''Personal reasons. I fell in love with her a long time ago and asked her to marry me. Only I walked away from all the wonderful things she offered me because I didn't want her to lead the empty life my mother had, raising children on her own while my dad chased his career like a lover pursuing a mistress.''

Hope slowly digested his words. ''So why the sudden change of heart?''

Quinn reddened. ''I recently found myself in circumstances that led me to realize how presumptuous my assumption had been about my mother's life. My life has been anything but empty since Kyle and Melanie needed me to be their daddy. This woman in the photo, she told me I'd broken her heart, and I'm hoping she'll give me the chance to repair it.''

Hope pushed the photo back toward him, nearly choking on the bitterness that welled in her. ''Why should she? You look like a man who breaks his promises. Maybe after you find her you'll decide she isn't what you want.''

He dropped down on his haunches so that their eyes met. ''I doubt that. In fact, I came very close to staying married to someone who looks a lot like this woman in the photo because I thought Kyle and Melanie needed a mother. But I couldn't do it, especially when I found out my wife might be in love with another man. I thought I had to let her find out who she wanted to be with and make her own choices.'' He tapped the photo and his voice grew husky. ''This is the woman I have in my heart. The one I love for her courage and her strength and the way she makes me feel. She's the one I want to be married to for the rest of my life.''

Hope stared at him in wonder as he took a small box from his pocket. ''I know this ring isn't much— you need a microscope to see the diamond—but I made a promise to you with this ring, and I'm offering to make good on that promise now. Will you stay married to me, Hope? I can't guarantee what the future will hold, but I can guarantee you a genuine marriage based on love if you'll agree to remain my wife.''

He slipped the engagement ring he'd given her ten years ago onto her finger.

It still fit, the diamond as bright as the promise Quinn was offering her.

Quinn's features hardened to stone. ''You aren't saying anything. Am I wrong about your feelings for me?''

Hope moistened her lips as tears filled her eyes. Quinn actually looked scared she would reject him. The part of her she'd thought scarred forever quivered with joy and trepidation. In the last few weeks, Quinn had become the man she'd always known he had the potential to be. And she had no doubt that he loved her. But was his idea of a genuine marriage in sync with hers? She didn't want any misunderstanding of their expectations of one another. Not this time. Her voice shook as she said flatly, "I want two more promises."

One black brow arched. "Two?"

"You have to promise to make love to me one hundred days straight. And I want a baby. Your baby."

The corners of his mouth twitched. "Well then, I suggest you go back inside and grab the suitcase and the envelope."

Her breath caught in her throat. "Why?"

"Don't ask questions. Just go look. And hurry, the kids are probably going stir-crazy in the car. I bribed them with marshmallows to keep them busy."

Hope raced into the house. Inside the envelope she found four airplane tickets to Hawaii and a voucher from Jolie promising to watch her day-care kids. When she unzipped the suitcase, she discovered enough wispy bits of lace and silk to adorn a sheik's harem. There wasn't a box of condoms in sight.

With a whoop of delight, she charged back onto the porch and flung herself into Quinn's arms. "I love you, Quinn McClure."

His warmth and strength encircled her as he dropped a heated kiss on her jaw and blazed a trail of fire to her temple. "Does this mean you're coming on the honeymoon with me?"

"Yes. Oh yes!"

Several satisfying kisses later, Quinn waited while Hope packed a few essentials. Then he swept her up in his arms—suitcase and all—and carried her to the car. As he slid Hope's suitcase into the trunk, he felt a light feathery brush on his cheek and heard the sound of his brother's husky laughter echo in his ears. *You done good, Quinn.*

Quinn smiled to himself. His brother always had to have the last word. For once, Quinn didn't mind a bit.

Shh!

HARLEQUIN®

I N T R I G U E®

has a secret…

September 2000

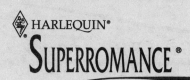

HARLEQUIN®
SUPERROMANCE®

You are now entering

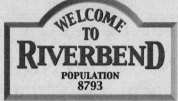

WELCOME
TO
RIVERBEND
POPULATION
8793

Riverbend...the kind of place where everyone knows
your name—and your business. Riverbend...home of
the River Rats—a group of small-town sons and
daughters who've been friends since high school.

The Rats are all grown up now. Living their lives and
learning that some days are good and some days
aren't—and that you can get through anything
as long as you have your friends.

Starting in July 2000, Harlequin Superromance brings
you Riverbend—six books about the River Rats and
the Midwest town they live in.

Available wherever Harlequin books are sold.

HARLEQUIN®
Makes any time special ™

Visit us at www.eHarlequin.com

HSRIVER

COMING NEXT MONTH

#573 THE STRANGER NEXT DOOR by Joanna Wayne
Randolph Family Ties

First a baby was left on the family's doorstep, then a beautiful woman with
no memory inherited the ranch next door. Langley Randolph wasn't sure
what was going on, but he intended to find out. Danger lurked, but the
passion aroused by his mysterious new neighbor, Danielle, made protecting
her his duty—and having her his heart's desire.

#574 INNOCENT WITNESS by Leona Karr

After witnessing a murder, Deanna Drake's four-year-old daughter was
traumatized into silence. With the help of Dr. Steve Sherman and his
young son, her daughter found her voice—and incited the killer to attack
again. But to get to Deanna and her daughter, the madman would have to
go through Steve first....

#575 BLACKMAILED BRIDE by Sylvie Kurtz

For two weeks, Cathlynn O'Connell agreed to play the role of wife to the
enigmatic researcher Jonas Shades. But alone in his secluded mansion,
what began as a temporary arrangement soon spiraled into an intricate
web of deceit, danger and disguised passions. Someone knew Cathlynn
was an impostor. What they didn't know was that Jonas intended to make
a proper bride of Cathlynn—if he could keep her alive.

#576 A MAN OF HONOR by Tina Leonard

Intuition told Cord Greer that things were not what they seemed. When
two men came in search of Tessa Draper, Cord's first instinct was to
protect. But now that the pregnant Tessa shared the intimacy of Cord's
solitary ranch, he had to rethink his actions. Someone was out there
watching, waiting to take away the only woman he'd ever loved and the
child he considered his own.

Visit us at www.eHarlequin.com

CNM0600